BEDTIME STORIES

From the Editors of Highlights for Children

BARNES
&NOBLE
BOOKS
NEW YORK

This edition published by Barnes & Noble, Inc.,
by arrangement with Boyds Mills Press, Inc.

Printed in Mexico

1994 Barnes & Noble Books
Book designed by Charlie Cary
The text of this book is set in 12-point Century Schoolbook.

ISBN 1-56619-613-2

10 9 8 7 6 5 4 3 2 1

CONTENTS

Turtle's Long Trip

By Bob Blaskey

The invitations came the day before Kitten's birthday.

"We must go," Bird said.

"Of course," said Goat. "Kitten is our best friend."

"But I cannot go," said Turtle. "I cannot walk that far."

The three friends lived at the bottom of a large hill. Kitten lived at the top. The only way to reach the top was a long trail that went up, up, up, up.

"Do you really want to go to Kitten's party?" Goat asked.

Turtle nodded.

"Then you are going," said Bird.

"But how?"

Bird shook her head. "Wait and see" was all she said.

The three went to sleep early so they could get up before dawn. The next morning they all stood at the bottom of the trail. Turtle looked up.

"It is too far for me," he said. "You go without me."

"Yes, it is far," Goat said. "But see if you can make it to that first turn in the trail."

"That seems easy enough," Turtle said. And he started off.

When they got to the first turn in the trail, Turtle was very tired. "I will stay here until you come back," he said.

Bird had an idea. She flew high in the air, then came down next to Turtle. "There are some fresh green leaves halfway up the hill," she said. "Just the kind you like to eat."

Turtle licked his lips. He was tired, but he was hungry, too. "I guess I can go a little farther."

So the three walked halfway up the hill to where the green leaves that Turtle liked to eat were growing. He ate and ate. When he was finished, he looked up. "I cannot go any farther. Just leave me here."

Goat said, "Walk with us just a little farther, Turtle. Tell us about the time you won the football game by hiding the ball in your shell."

Turtle started telling about the game. As he talked, he walked along with his friends. By the time he was finished, they could almost see the top of the hill.

"I did not know we had come so far," said Turtle. "I forgot all about being tired while we were talking. But I really cannot go the rest of the way." He pulled his head into his shell.

"Come back out!" said Bird. "You can do it!"

"No, I cannot," Turtle said, popping out again.

"Yes, you can," Bird answered. "One step at a time. First one foot, then the other."

Turtle shook his head. "I cannot," he said. But he put out his foot.

"Yes, you can," Goat said.

"No, I cannot," Turtle said, taking another step.

"Yes, you can," said Bird.

Turtle kept shaking his head and saying he could not make it, but he kept on walking.

Suddenly, there were Kitten and the other animals. They were at the top!

Turtle was tired but he felt good. "I did it," he said. He looked at Goat and Bird. "With a little help from my friends."

Then they all went to the party.

A Teddy Bear for

By Bonnie Highsmith Taylor

Teddy lived in a snug, warm cave with Mother and Father Bear. He loved his forest home and was happy there.

He ate wild berries. He caught fish from the streams. He dug juicy grubworms from rotten logs. He was fat, and his coat was sleek and shiny.

For fun, he climbed trees and turned somersaults down hills. Teddy was a very contented bear. But then he met a real teddy bear.

It was a bright summer morning. Teddy lumbered along, sniffing the good forest smells. Suddenly, he stopped short. In the clearing just ahead was a camp with people—a man, a woman, and a small boy.

Teddy had seen people before. But he had never seen anything like what the small boy was holding in his arms. It had a brown fur coat. Just like a bear. It had a short, stubby tail. Just like a bear. It had small black eyes. Just like a bear. And when the boy squeezed its body, it went *OOF!* Just like a bear.

Teddy watched in wonder. How he would love to have one of those for his very own!

That night when Teddy told his mother about it, she said, "It must be a toy. Children are fond of toys that look like animals."

Teddy almost wished he were a little boy, for he had never seen anything he wanted so badly.

The next morning he crept carefully through the trees to the edge of the same clearing. The camp was still there, but the man and woman and little boy were gone. Teddy was disappointed. When he turned to leave, he spied the toy bear lying on a stump.

In no time at all Teddy was holding it in his arms. He squeezed it till it went *OOF!* He rubbed the soft fur with his paw. He was so interested in playing with the toy that he didn't hear the people returning to the camp.

"Look! Look!" cried the little boy. "A bear! A real, live bear! And he's playing with my teddy bear!"

Teddy was so frightened that he dropped the toy bear and ran all the way back to his cave.

Teddy Bear

But he couldn't stay away. The very next morning he was back again. This time the people had taken a long hike up a mountain and were gone until nearly dark. Teddy spent the whole day playing with the wonderful toy. When the people came back, he hid in the bushes and watched the little boy get ready for bed. Teddy sighed when the little boy took the toy bear inside the tent. How nice to have something so soft to sleep with!

Every day Teddy made his way back to the camp. When the people were there, he stayed hidden and watched the boy play with the little bear.

But one morning when Teddy arrived as usual, his heart sank. The camp was gone! The car, the tent, everything! Teddy sat down and cried. How he would miss the little toy bear.

After a long time he got up and started slowly toward the stream. Tears filled his eyes till he could hardly see where he was going.

Suddenly, he tripped on something. He looked down. The toy bear! The little boy had left it behind.

There was a note tied around its neck, but, of course, Teddy could not read it. It said

> Dear Bear,
> Please keep my teddy bear.
> I have three more at home.
> > Your friend,
> > Bobby

Teddy clutched the wonderful toy in his paws and hurried home to show it to his mother.

Go to Sleep, Devi

By Marileta Robinson

A long time ago, when the world was new, a woman named Nyonu and a man named Nutsu had a baby girl named Devi. She was a happy baby. She never gave her mother and father much trouble.

But one night Devi could not go to sleep. No matter what her mother and father tried, Devi cried and cried. Was she hungry? No. Was she sick? No. She was just too sleepy to sleep, and so she cried.

"What are we going to do?" said Nyonu. "She will keep the whole forest awake."

Sure enough, the birds heard the baby's crying and came to help. They sat around the baby's bed and sang their sweetest songs. But Devi just cried louder.

The monkey came with a handful of the baby's favorite fruit. Still she cried. The elephant brought a trunkful of sweet-smelling hay for the baby's bed. Devi howled.

The lion brought her little cubs. They looked so funny scrambling and tumbling over each other that she thought the baby might laugh. But Devi just kept on crying.

Then Nyonu picked up Devi and walked back and forth, back and forth. Devi stopped crying, but she did not go to sleep. Nyonu stopped to rest. "Waah!" cried Devi.

"Oh, dear," said Nyonu. "I cannot walk back and forth, back and forth, without stopping. What shall I do?"

Nutsu took Devi from her, and he walked back and forth. Nyonu sat down to rest. But she could not sit still. Her body rocked back and forth, back and forth. As he walked with the baby, Nutsu watched Nyonu rocking. When it was Nyonu's turn to walk the baby again, Nutsu said, "I'm going to try something. I will be right back."

Nutsu went outside and got some poles and some vines. He tied them together to make a seat with legs and a back. Then he took two curved elephant tusks he had been saving, cut holes in them, and stuck the legs of the seat into the holes. Then he carried the thing he had made for Nyonu to see.

Nyonu gave him an odd look.

"Sit down," said Nutsu. "Try it out."

Nyonu sat down in the seat with Devi. The seat rocked back and forth, back and forth. Nyonu smiled. Nutsu smiled. Soon Devi was sound asleep.

The Ogre and the Monkey King

A Tale of Ancient India

By Josepha Sherman

Long, long ago, a troop of monkeys went traveling through the jungle. There were big monkeys and little monkeys, old monkeys and tiny baby monkeys. Sometimes they ran on the ground, and sometimes they swung by their arms and tails through the trees. All of them followed their wise old monkey king.

But why were they traveling? Was it for fun?

Oh no.

No rain had fallen in the jungle, no rain at all for a long, long time. The little pools and streams near the monkeys' home had all dried up. And the monkeys were looking for a place where there was water for all of them. They were looking for a place where they could stay until the rains came again.

But they couldn't find water. They were tired, and all of them were very thirsty.

"Oh, wait!" cried one young monkey. "I think I smell water. Yes, I do."

10

"So do I," cried another monkey. "And look! There is a lake."

It was a big lake. It was a beautiful lake, very blue and very clear.

"We have water!" cried the monkeys. "We can stay here."

And they all started to run out of the jungle toward the lake. Suddenly the wise old monkey king shouted, "Stop! You must not go near the lake! You must not drink!"

"Why not?" asked an angry monkey.

"We're thirsty," said another. "All of us are thirsty. We want to drink."

"Why should we stop?" cried all the monkeys.

"Look," said their king. "Look at the edge of the lake. What do you see?"

"Tracks," they said. "We see animal tracks. Other animals drink at the lake. Why can't we drink, too?"

"Don't you see? Look again. All the tracks lead to the lake, but none of the tracks lead away from the lake."

"Yes," cried the monkeys, "we see. But what can it mean?"

"Something lives in that lake—something that eats animals. Let us wait," said the king. "Let us wait away from the lake and watch to see what will happen."

11

They waited, and suddenly the lake waters thrashed and splashed. The monkeys were afraid. What lived in that lake?

It was an ogre!—an ugly monster with light blue skin and dark red eyes and sharp teeth. And it was very hungry. The ogre wanted to eat the monkeys, but it couldn't get out of the lake to reach them. So it pretended to smile at them.

"Why are you sitting out there?" the ogre asked, trying to make its rough voice sound soft and pretty. "This water is pure. This water is sweet. Aren't you thirsty? You must be thirsty. Come and drink. I will not hurt you."

"Oh no," said the monkey king. "You don't fool us. You want us to come to you because you can't get out of the lake. You want us to come to you so you can eat us! But we won't let you."

"But what can we do?" asked a little monkey. "I am so very thirsty. I don't think I can walk any farther."

"We are all very thirsty," agreed a mother monkey. "And my baby is too tiny to travel anymore. We must have water. We must have this water!"

"Yes," said the monkey king sadly. "I know. We will have this water, but I will not let the ogre eat any of us. Let me think."

He looked at the lake. He looked at the ogre. He looked at the long reeds growing all around the lake.

And at last the monkey king began to smile.

"Why are you smiling?" asked the puzzled ogre. "You are tired. You are thirsty. Why are you smiling?"

"I am smiling because we are going to drink from your lake. We are going to drink from your lake—but you will not be able to eat any of us."

"How can that be?" asked the monkeys. "We can drink only if we go right up to the edge of the lake. And if we go right up to the edge of the lake, the ogre will be able to catch us."

"Wait," said their king. "You will see. Come, my swiftest young monkeys. Gather reeds. Gather enough reeds so that each of us can have one."

The young monkeys obeyed. They ran. They gathered reeds. Soon they brought back enough for all the monkeys.

Then all the monkeys saw how they would drink. They knew how wise their king had been.

Those long reeds were hollow. They were hollow as straws!

So each monkey dipped a hollow reed into the lake and drank the cool water while the ogre shouted and shouted. The reeds were too long! The ogre couldn't catch a single monkey. They were safe.

And the wise old monkey king smiled happily.

The Greedy Frog

An Aboriginal legend from Australia retold by Priscilla P. Moore

In the Dreamtime, when the world began, giant creatures walked the land. One of the biggest was a green frog called Gruggum.

Gruggum was so enormous that whenever he hopped, the ground shivered and the trees shook. Unlike frogs today, Gruggum did not live in water, because no river was large enough to hold him.

One day when there was not a whiff of air and the hot land simmered in the sun, all the animals gathered at a water hole to drink and to gossip. As Possum was complaining that he couldn't remember a longer spell without rain, the earth began to shake and the leaves of the gum trees whispered a warning.

"Gruggum is coming!" shouted a baby kangaroo from his mother's pouch.

The animals scattered as the giant frog hopped up to the water hole and began to drink. *Glug. Glug. Glug.* In three big gulps Gruggum drained the water hole, leaving only a mud hole behind.

It was such a hot day and Gruggum was such

a big frog that he was still thirsty. He hopped to a river and slurped and slurped until the river disappeared.

The animals began to worry. "Gruggum is drinking all the water," whispered Dingo the dog.

"There will be nothing left for us," agreed Goanna the lizard.

Gruggum did not care. He hopped down to the ocean and drank and drank.

"Gruggum, stop!" begged a bottle-nosed dolphin.

But the giant frog did not stop. He swallowed the ocean. Then he hopped from water hole to stream to lake, until there was nothing left to drink.

Gruggum, his stomach swollen with all the earth's water, hopped to the top of the highest mountain. With his lips pressed together, he stared unblinking across the dry land.

"What will we do?" asked Koala, peeking through the leaves of a gum tree.

"We must think of a way to make Gruggum give back the water," said Tortoise.

"Let's scare him," suggested Dingo.

"How can you scare someone as big as Gruggum?" asked the ground-burrowing Wombat. "We should tickle him. When he laughs, the water will pour out of his mouth."

"Gruggum is too big. We cannot reach high enough to tickle him," said the dark-feathered Kookaburra.

All the animals turned to wise old Kangaroo. "What shall we do?" they chorused.

"Wombat's suggestion was good," said Kangaroo. "If we can make Gruggum laugh, he will have to open his mouth. We must think of something to make him laugh."

"You try, Kookaburra," said Wombat. "Laughing is what you do best."

Everyone agreed that no one could laugh as gaily as Kookaburra. His loud chuckle often filled the bushland.

"Ha, ha, ha, ha. Ho, ho, ho, ho," Kookaburra laughed merrily. Soon all the animals were laughing with him. But not Gruggum. His lips remained sealed, his eyes unblinking.

"Let me try," begged the big bird, Emu. "I will walk my silliest walk. Surely Gruggum will laugh at me." Emu bounced along on his spindly legs. His long neck bobbed up and down. He was so gawky that soon all the animals, including Emu, were giggling. But Gruggum never even smiled.

"Emu was funny," said a frisky young kangaroo. "But watch me hop.

I'll make that big frog laugh."

He bounced up to another kangaroo, and the two began chasing one another. They hopped over bushes, sideways and backward. Finally, one did a backflip right into the other. They both landed flat in the dust. All the animals shouted with glee.

But not Gruggum. He sat on his mountain, plump from all the earth's water. The corners of his mouth never twitched.

"Maybe frogs don't laugh," suggested Goanna.

Two thin eels wriggled forward. "Frogs do laugh," said one.

"We've seen them," said the second eel.

"We can make this greedy frog laugh," said the first eel.

The two eels wriggled and began to dance. They slithered and slid this way and that, curling and furling side by side. Two eels on dry land did look silly trying to dance. All the animals smiled. Gruggum watched, but he did not smile.

Suddenly, the eels twisted together like two strands of fishing line. They had tied themselves into a knot.

"Let go of my tail!" screeched one eel.

"Let go of mine!" shouted the other.

The more they tried to untie themselves, the tighter they knotted together. Finally, from the tangle came a thin, reedy cry, "Help! Oh, help!"

The animals burst into laughter. Even the flies buzzed with glee. Never had they seen anything so funny as those two eels tied together.

"Look!" shouted Wombat. "That greedy frog is smiling." All the animals turned to Gruggum. A wide grin stretched across his big green face. As they watched, the frog began to chuckle. Water trickled from the corners of his mouth. Finally, he roared with a deep belly-shaking laugh, and all the earth's water poured forth.

The water ran back into the water holes, lakes, and ponds. It filled the rivers and streams. Once again the blue-green ocean shimmered in the sun. The animals were grateful, especially to the eels.

"You two saved the day," said wise old Kangaroo.

"We told you that frogs laugh," they said together. "Now please untie us!"

The animals untangled the eels, and they slithered into the nearest river. As for Gruggum the greedy frog, never again did he swallow all the earth's water.

The Man in the Moon

By Thomas Sarmo

More than anything, Robin missed his old home. He missed it as he watched his father unpack his clock. He missed it as his mother began to fill his new bookshelves.

No one else seemed sad. No one else missed the country.

"There's a lot to see here," said his father. "You'll like the city, Rob."

"We always make the best of things," said his mother.

Robin thought of his old room. He had loved to watch the moon rise as he leaned out the window. It would light up the water on the curves of the river. It would shine silver on the roof of the courthouse steeple.

"I miss that," whispered Robin.

It was dusk. Robin went out on the front porch, looking for the moon. A very old man with a round face sat on the curb. He pointed to a parked car and sighed.

"I've lost something," said the man sadly. "And I'm not where I should be." He glanced up at the moonless sky.

Robin looked under the car. A light shone underneath.

"It's my silver piece," said the man, rubbing his eyes. "And I'm too old to crawl under."

Robin lay on his stomach and reached. He handed the coin to the man, and it seemed to shine more brightly. The old man stood up to leave.

"You're new here," he said. "And you're sad."

"I miss my home," said Robin. "It was in the country." He felt his throat thicken. "And I miss the river," he added.

"The river . . . ," said the old man thoughtfully. "It's a quiet river, right, with big curves?"

"You know it?" asked Robin. "One big curve turns round the courthouse."

"There's a bell in the steeple," said the man. "And the roof shines silver—"

"In the moonlight," said Robin. "I could see it from my bedroom."

"It's a fine place," said the man, sitting down again. "I don't blame you for missing it."

"But we have to make the best of things," said Robin. He hung his head. "My mom says that."

"You can still miss the river," said the old man.

"And the courthouse bell," said Robin.

"You can see the moon anyplace," said the man.

Robin looked up. The city lights sparkled. Orange windows shone from dark buildings.

"It is kind of pretty here," said Robin. "But I don't see the moon."

"You'll see it," said the old man. He held up the silvery coin. "And when you see it, remember that it's shining on your old home, too."

"I won't forget," said Robin.

The old man walked down the street and out of sight. Robin turned and saw the moon, rising up from behind his new house. Moonlight floated down his street, now shining silver as the water in a river.

Right in the Middle of the King's Highway

By Margaret Walden Froehlich

Once upon a time a hen and a duck were on their way to Mayberry Fair when they saw something round lying right in the middle of the King's Highway. "I do not know what it is," said the hen. "But it is making a sound, so it must be alive."

"Let's move it to the side of the road," said the duck. "Horses and carriages could run over it here."

"Oh no," answered the hen. "Let's not touch it. It might bite."

So, to warn the horses and carriages not to run over the round thing right in the middle of the King's Highway, the hen and the duck picked some flowers from a bush at the side of the road and placed them in a circle around the thing.

"Now it is safe," said the hen. "Let's go to the fair."

"But look at the poor little thing," said the duck. "The sun is shining so brightly on its back. We should put something over it to keep it from getting too hot."

The hen and the duck hurried back home and got a chair.

"That is better," they both said after they had placed the chair

carefully over the round thing right in the middle of the King's Highway.

Just then along came a cat on his way to the fair. The sound the little round thing was making interested the cat. He jumped up on the chair to listen to it. "This is an interesting creature," said the cat. "Maybe I will learn something from it."

The hen and the duck thought that was a good idea. They decided to stay awhile and listen, too.

With the cat's help they brought more chairs and settled down to listen.

A dog on her way to the fair was surprised to see them all sitting right in the middle of the King's Highway. When they told her what they were doing, she decided to join the group. First, though, she put up an awning to keep them shady and comfortable.

By and by a pig came by. After he heard what was going on, the pig said, "I would stay and listen, too, if there were something here to eat."

"What a sensible idea," said the hen, and she went to fetch a basket of food.

"How nice," said the cat, and he found some sticks to make a nice little cupboard to hold the food.

"Wonderful idea," said the dog, who bought some bricks from a wagon passing by and built a little house all around the chairs and the cupboard right in the middle of the King's Highway.

"There's just one more thing we need," said the duck, and she dipped up a pan of nice clear water from the brook and brought it along to keep them from getting thirsty.

The pig offered a drop of water and a bit of corn to the thing under the cat's chair. "Its throat must be dry from talking all the time," he said.

Along came a horse at a gallop. She almost knocked over the house in her hurry to get to the fair. "What in the world is this right in the middle of the King's Highway?" she shouted.

"Sh-h-h," warned the animals. "We are trying to listen."

They told the horse to stick her head through the window and listen to the thing under the cat's chair.

"Remarkable," said the horse. "If there were room, I would stay and listen, too."

Everyone helped build a turret to the house so the horse would have room for her head. They cut the striped awning into banners and flew them from the turret.

The horse joined them in listening.

They listened and listened until their ears got tired. Then they went

outside to rest and stretch their legs.

While they were walking about, the sound of trumpets was heard, and round the bend came the king's golden carriage. The coachman pulled the horses to a stop, and out of the carriage came the king shouting, "What is this? Who has built a castle right in the middle of the King's Highway?"

The queen poked her head out the window of the coach to find out what was happening. "Look at your watch, and tell me what time it is," she said to the king. "I am afraid we will be late for Mayberry Fair."

"Oh, me," exclaimed the king when he put his hand in his waistcoat pocket and found that his watch was missing. "First this building is right in the middle of my highway, and now my watch is lost!"

Immediately, all the king's men started to search for the missing watch. The animals gathered around the king.

"What is wrong?" they asked. "May we be of help?"

"It is round," explained the king. "It goes tick, tick . . ."

"Oh, my," interrupted the dog. She ran and fetched the round thing from under the chair.

"We thought your watch was an animal of some sort," said the cat.

"And we made a shelter to keep it safe," the duck and the hen added.

"Ah," said the king as he put the watch into his pocket. "To show my thanks, I will leave the building that sheltered my watch right here in the middle of the highway. Travelers can use it as a place to stop and rest. And now, how would all of you like to come with me to the fair?"

"Oh yes," cried the animals. They climbed aboard the carriage, and off they all went to Mayberry Fair.

The Bear Who Did Not Like Honey

By Nancy Buss

Robert was afraid of bees. His mother did not know. "She would think I am silly," Robert mumbled. "No bees, no honey," she would say.

But Robert knew that. And Robert liked honey better than anything—although he pretended not to. For if he said he did not like honey, then he did not have to help his sister, Beverly, fill the honey jar. And if he did not have to help fill the honey jar, he could stay away from bees. And that was just fine with Robert.

Robert's father did not know his secret either. "He would be angry," Robert muttered. "Bees cannot hurt you," his father would say. "You are all covered with fur."

Robert knew that. But he was still afraid. He jumped if a bee zoomed near him. He ran if he heard bees buzzing in a meadow. And he yelped and covered his nose if a bee landed near him. "There is no fur on my nose," he said to himself.

He kept his secret safe. He kept it safe from his sister. He kept it safe from his cousin Howard. And he kept it safe from his grandpa. But most of all he kept it safe from his friends. "They would laugh at me," he said to himself. "Robert is a baby, Robert is a baby," they would yell—if they knew. But no one knew. And Robert became known as the bear who did not like honey.

"I just do not care for any," he would say when his mother passed the honey jar. Beverly got to finish it all.

"No, thank you," he would say when his grandma offered him a honey cake. He ate a carrot instead.

But it was worse when he was with his friends.

"Oh, yuck!" he would say when they found a hive filled with bees and honey. "You guys are going to get sick eating all that stuff," he would call from a safe distance. But his friends never got sick. They just ate and ate and ate till all the honey was gone. And Robert had to watch.

All these things made Robert angry. "It is not fair!" he said to himself. "EVERYBODY gets honey but ME!" And Robert became a grump. He fought with his sister. He snapped at his friends. He became so unpleasant that no one wanted to play with him. He spent most of the day up in his room thinking about honey. And every night he had the same dream. There, in the middle of the forest, was a tree filled with honey. There were no bees. They had all disappeared. Robert ate and ate and ate.

One night Robert woke up, still licking the dream honey from his paw.

"I must have some honey!" he said as he crept from his bed. "Now!"

Robert tiptoed down the hall to the kitchen. He climbed up on a chair, opened the cupboard, and reached for the honey. He took one big gulp, then another, and another. The honey dribbled down his chin onto his stomach and his toes. It was almost like his dream. Robert had not been so happy in a very long time.

"Robert, whatever are you doing?" asked his mother.

"I thought you were a thief," said his father.

"Robert is eating honey," Beverly said.

"Robert is eating what?" asked Mother and Father.

"Honey!" said Robert. "I love honey!"

"But we thought you hated it."

So Robert explained. And when his secret was told, he felt much better. His mother did not think he was silly at all. And his father was not angry.

"You will not always be afraid," he said to Robert. "You will grow a little, and soon you will forget all about being afraid of bees. I promise."

But Robert was right about his friends. Beverly could not keep a secret. And when she told them, they laughed and giggled and hooted and shrieked till Robert turned and started to walk away.

"Wait," Beverly called. She had not meant to hurt his feelings. "I know some other secrets, too. Arthur is afraid of mice, and Rachel is afraid of climbing trees, and William is afraid of the water . . . and I am afraid of the dark." She said the last in a very small voice.

"But that is silly," Robert said. "I am not afraid of any of those things."

"No," said Arthur. "Mostly you are a very brave bear. And I am sorry I made fun of you." All of the others agreed.

And mostly Robert *was* brave. Oh, he still jumped if a bee zoomed too close. He still did not help with the honey jar. But he grew a little, just as his father said he would. And one day, when Robert was out in the woods, a bee landed right on Robert's nose. Robert was surprised. But he did not holler. He did not yelp. He just brushed the bee off his nose and went down the road, whistling.

Noodletoo

By B.L. Dickinson

I was bored. There was nothing to do. Mom gave me a long piece of red yarn and some large macaroni noodles. I decided to make a noodle necklace with them. Mom said she would help me put the yarn through the noodles if I had trouble with it. I thought I could do it.

I wonder if there are noodles everywhere. I wonder if there are noodles on the Moon. I asked my mom when she came to tie a knot in the yarn. She put the necklace over my head and said she didn't think there were noodles in space. I told her I'm going to pretend there are. She told me to use my noodle and have a good time.

I'll pretend I'm going on an adventure to another planet! Which planet? Not Pluto. Too cold. Not Venus. Too hot. I'll take a trip to NOODLETOO! A make-believe trip can be to a make-believe place.

I'll put on my astronaut suit. Zip it up. Now my space boots. Lace them up. Last of all, my helmet. There, I'm ready for takeoff.

I crawl under the table and into my spaceship.

Ten, nine, eight, seven, six, five, four, three, two, one, blast-off! NOODLETOO, here I come!

I can see a steamy planet through my spaceship window. It must be NOODLETOO because when we cook noodles, they make steam.

I'm coming in for a landing! Ten, nine, eight, seven, six, five, four, three, two, one, splooshdown!

I'm stepping out of my rocket and putting my feet in . . . noodles! Soft, steamy pasta. I can see spaghetti, lasagna, fettucini, all kinds of pasta, everywhere. I sniff the warm breeze. It smells like cheese and tomato sauce. Yummy!

I wonder if anyone lives on this planet. Wait . . . what's this? I see a box on a large, flat lasagna noodle. I walk and bounce over to it. It looks like a lunch box. There is a name on it—Mac A. Roni. Someone named Mac must live here.

I hear noises. I hear voices. My heart is beating on my ribs. I'm afraid. What if the voices are coming from monsters? Space monsters! NOODLETOO monsters! I hide behind a large pasta shell. The voices are louder. They don't sound like monster voices. They sound like children . . . happy children.

I move to the other side of the shell and peek around the edge. Oh, my! I see little pasta people playing in a playground. They are swinging on linguine and sliding down huge pieces of ruffled lasagna.

I hear someone call, "Resauce is over. Time to come inside." The little pasta people are running at me! Wait . . . no . . . they are not after me. They are disappearing into their pasta shell.

I put my ear against the pasta wall. I can hear someone say, "Take out your pencils and paper, class." This must be a school. I lean around the corner of the shell. I can see a sort of doorway. There is a sign hanging by pieces of spaghetti. The sign says Elbow Room.

I move back behind the pasta. I know it's OK to be different, but this place is super strange. I guess these pasta people would think Earth is strange, too.

"Hey, Mac!"

What's that? Someone's coming! I jump and slide into a huge manicotti tunnel.

"Wait up, Mac. You forgot your lunch box."

Two little pasta people walk past me. Whew, they didn't notice me hiding in here.

"Thanks. My mom would have been upset if I forgot it again."

"Yeah. I know what you mean. Is there meatball practice today?"

"The coach said there would be practice if it doesn't sprinkle."

"Aw, a little Parmesan never hurt anyone. I hope we don't have to cancel."

"Me, too. I have to get home. See you."

"'Bye."

That's really weird! Meatball practice? Parmesan rain? This is too much. I think I'd better get back to Earth.

I crawl out of the big noodle and sneak back to my spaceship. Ten, nine, eight, seven, six, five, four, three, two, one, blast-off! Goodbye, NOODLETOO . . . Hello, Earth.

My spaceship lands safely under the table. It's good to be home. Mom says, "Welcome back. Go wash up for dinner. We're having your favorite—spaghetti."

I wonder if pasta people ever take pretend trips to Earth.

Lisa's Kid

By Janet D. Chiefari

"**M**om, I hear Daisy!" shouted Lisa. "The kid is coming. I know it's time."

Mom quickly walked into the kitchen. She and Lisa could indeed hear the goat bleating through the intercom that was connected to the barn.

Daisy was a few days past her expected delivery date. Dad had talked about his concern for the pregnant doe and her kid that morning at the breakfast table. He had told Lisa not to worry.

But Lisa *had* worried. Daisy was Lisa's favorite of the three goats that made up the family's small dairy herd. Daisy's kid, her first kid, was going to be so special. It was to be Lisa's birthday present, hers to care for and love.

Waiting five months for the baby goat had been a hard thing for Lisa to do. Dad said, "Nature has to take its own time." So Lisa had used the time to plan and prepare for the kid's arrival. She had asked her mom and dad many questions about caring for the newborn animal. She had helped her dad build Daisy a kidding pen—a special place to have her baby. She had even chosen a name—"Honey"—because the taste of honey was as sweet a treat as the kid would be.

Finally the moment was arriving, and Lisa was so excited. She grabbed her jacket from its special hook on the wall by the door. She counted the steps to the barn and was there before her mother. Opening the door to the kidding pen, she heard Daisy bleating. Reaching out, she patted the goat. Daisy's fur was short and coarse, yet soft when Lisa's fingertips slid underneath. Lisa hugged the goat's large rounded sides and stroked her small pointed ears.

"It's going to be all right, Daisy," she said.

Arriving breathlessly, Mom checked the doe.

"It won't be long now," she said.

Lisa sat down in the corner of the pen on a bale of hay. She could feel the warm spring sun shining through the window, and she could smell the sweetness of warm hay. Summer would soon be here, and she would have Honey as her very own.

Suddenly Mom said, "Here it comes!" Then Lisa heard the cries of the little newborn animal.

Lisa gave Daisy a few minutes to greet her new baby. Then she jumped to the floor, and her mother handed her the tiny bundle of wet fur and a large soft towel to dry it with. Cuddling the animal in her lap, Lisa rubbed and rubbed until the baby's hair was soft and fluffy. Her fingers felt the kid's thin legs, then carefully traced the animal's head, ears, and nose. The baby sucked at Lisa's fingertips.

"Is it a doe or a buck?" Lisa asked.

"A beautiful little doe," Mom said.

Lisa was pleased. Another doe was a welcome addition to the herd. Soon there would be four milking does to provide milk and cheese for the family.

Beaming a huge smile, Lisa asked, "What color is she?"

"She's a warm golden color, just like honey. You chose the perfect name for her."

Lisa gently patted the little animal she would never see but would know and love in many other ways.

Bumpo Loses His Nose

By Marilyn Kratz

Bumpo the clown reached into a drawer for his big red nose, but it wasn't there. He quickly searched the dressing room, but he couldn't find the funny red nose anywhere.

Just then he heard the circus band beginning to play.

"The parade is starting!" he cried, running to the big tent. The other clowns were already tumbling along in the colorful parade of acrobats, lion tamers, elephants, and other performers and animals, all dressed in their sparkling bright costumes.

Bumpo ran up to the clowns. "Has anyone seen my big red nose?" he shouted, pointing to his own little white nose.

But the clowns were just getting ready to do their firecracker trick. They couldn't stop to help Bumpo.

"Maybe one of those pesky monkeys took it," said Bumpo, running at full speed to the monkey cage at one side of the big tent.

The monkeys jumped about and chattered as Bumpo ran around their cage, searching for his nose. Suddenly, one of the monkeys grabbed Bumpo's fancy hat. The monkey put the hat on his head and danced merrily about.

"I can get along without my hat," Bumpo decided. "But I must find that nose." He ran to the side ring to search in the bucket of balls used in the seals' act.

But Bumpo was running so fast he couldn't stop. He tipped over the bucket of balls. They rolled about, tripping Bumpo every time he tried to stand up.

Luckily, the elephants were passing by. Raja, the biggest and friendliest elephant, reached over with his trunk and picked up Bumpo. Raja lifted Bumpo high in the air and then set him down gently—right in the middle of a cart filled with yipping dogs!

Bumpo jumped out of the cart. The startled dogs jumped out, too. They chased Bumpo around the center ring.

"Come back here with my dogs!" screamed the dog trainer, chasing after them.

Bumpo turned to shout, "I'm just trying to find my nose!" The toe of his raggedy shoe caught on the tightrope walker's pole, which was lying on the ground. Bumpo stumbled. He let himself tumble smoothly into a somersault and landed with his head poking through a paper-covered hoop used in the dog act.

"I just wanted to find my big red rubber nose," Bumpo moaned. He sat there in the middle of the center ring with his head in his hands.

At that moment Mr. Higgins, the ringmaster, ran up to Bumpo. "That's the best act you've ever done!" he shouted.

"Act?" said Bumpo. "What act?"

"The 'looking for your nose' act," said Mr. Higgins. "Just listen to the boys and girls."

Bumpo looked up. The children were all laughing and cheering and clapping for him.

Bumpo stood up and took a bow. As he did, his big red rubber nose popped out of his pocket and rolled across the circus ring. The children laughed harder than ever.

Bumpo picked up the big red rubber nose and stuck it to his face. Then he laughed and said, "I'm going to lose this nose every day!"

Rupert and the Royal Bread

The king shook his head, pulled his beard, and stamped his royal foot. "This has to stop," he cried. "Every time I look for Prince Rupert, he has disappeared. He should be working in the royal wheat fields."

The queen sighed. "I have the same problem with Princess Augusta. She disappears every time she should be in the royal kitchen."

"Send for the wizard," said Prince Henry, their royal uncle.

"Send for the wisewomen," cried the queen.

"Send for all of them," shouted the king.

Rupert came first, flour covering his arms. He was followed by Augusta, a rake over her shoulder.

The wisewomen and the royal wizard looked at Prince Rupert.

"Rupert should be in the wheat fields," said the first wisewoman.

"He is a prince. He should not be in the royal kitchen," said the second wisewoman.

"Send him from the kitchen to the fields," said the third wisewoman.

The wisewomen and the wizard looked at Princess Augusta.

"Augusta should be in the kitchen," said the first wisewoman.

"She is a princess. She should not be in the wheat fields," said the second wisewoman.

"Send her from the wheat fields to the royal kitchen," said the third wisewoman.

"I must study this problem," muttered the wizard.

Rupert shook his arms. Flour flew around the room. "I do not like to work in the royal wheat fields. I like to work in the royal kitchen," he shouted.

Augusta waved the rake. Everyone moved out of her way. "I do not like to work in the royal kitchen. I like to work in the royal wheat fields," she shouted.

"Stop! Stop! Stop!" yelled the king. "Rupert, you are a prince. You must work in the royal wheat fields. Augusta, you are a princess. You must work in the royal kitchen."

"Yes," said the wisewomen.

"I believe so," said the wizard.

"Why?" asked Prince Rupert. "Is it one of the royal laws?"

"Send for the royal lawbooks," cried the wizard. "I shall look and see."

The wizard studied the royal lawbooks.

"Hmmmm," said the wizard.

"Aha," said the wizard.

"This is very interesting," said the wizard.

"Did you find the law?" asked the king. "What does it say?"

The wizard put down the royal lawbooks. "There is no law. There is no rule. Nowhere is it written that Prince Rupert must work in the royal wheat fields. Nowhere is it written that Princess Augusta must work in the royal kitchen."

"No rule!" said the king in surprise. He cupped his head in his hands. "I must study this." He looked at Prince Rupert. He looked at Princess Augusta. Then he smiled.

"Princess Augusta, you may return to the royal wheat fields," said the king. He turned to Rupert. "Let's go," he said.

"Where are you going?" asked the queen.

"To the royal kitchen," said the king. "If there is no rule against a prince working in the kitchen, there will be no rule against a king working in the kitchen. I have always wanted to bake some whole wheat bread."

And he did.

How to Grow a Bicycle

By John and Linda Grimes

Rachel Lynn's father sat reading the newspaper in his special big chair in the den. Rachel came and sat next to him.

"Daddy," she said, "will you buy me a new bicycle?"

"A new bicycle!" Rachel's father exclaimed, laying the newspaper aside. "No, I will not buy you a new bicycle—but I will show you how to grow one."

Rachel looked confused and shook her head. She said, "You cannot grow a bicycle."

"Yes, you can," her father replied. "I used to grow all sorts of things when I was a little boy. If I needed a new baseball glove, a kite, or anything else, I grew it."

This sounded to Rachel like one of her father's tall tales. Her father could see that she did not believe him, so he said, "Rachel, if you really want a bicycle and are willing to work hard, I promise I will show you how to grow one."

"When do we start?" Rachel asked.

"We will start tomorrow," her father answered. "Now, you go to bed. You will need a lot of rest if you are going to grow a bicycle."

After breakfast Rachel and her father went into the backyard to begin growing the bicycle. Rachel watched while Father dug up a large area. It seemed to Rachel that it took a lot of ground to grow one bicycle.

After breaking up the ground, Rachel's father showed her how to mark the rows. It took a lot of rows to grow a bicycle. Then Rachel's father gave her the bicycle seeds. The seeds were flat and black. There were a lot of them, too.

Rachel asked her father, "How many bicycles are we growing?"

"Just one," he answered. He showed her how to put the seeds in each row and cover them with a thin layer of dirt. When Rachel was finished, she sat down to rest. Her father was right. It was hard work growing a bicycle!

For the next three months Rachel had to water her bicycle plants every few days, unless it rained. She had to keep the weeds out of the rows and the bugs off the plants.

Week after week Rachel watched the plants grow and grow. The plants did not look anything like a bicycle to Rachel—but her father had promised. She continued to water and weed the plants, which were looking more and more like watermelons.

Then one day Rachel's father said, "It's time to pick your bicycle."

They went into the backyard, and Rachel looked at the plants.

"There is no bicycle here, Daddy."

"Trust me," he answered, and he began picking the watermelon-looking things off the plants. He loaded them into the back of his truck. Then Rachel and her father drove to the farmers' market. A man helped unload the watermelons and gave Rachel's father some money.

Rachel's father drove to a store where Rachel picked out a shiny blue bicycle. They gave the money to the storekeeper, who gave Rachel a brand new bicycle.

Rachel gave her father a big hug. "Daddy," she said proudly, "you told me that I could grow a bicycle, and I sure did."

Always Room for

By Jan Tincher

Christopher

Arnold knew Mr. Jensen liked him because he often said so. But Arnold thought Mr. Jensen's heart must be crowded.

"Oh, my," said Mr. Jensen. "I have so many grandchildren that it is hard to keep count."

Arnold knew just how many grandchildren Mr. Jensen had. He had counted their pictures.

"Mr. Jensen has twenty-four grandchildren," he told his mom. "I even know their names." Then Arnold named them. All twenty-four of them. And at the very end he said, ". . . and Arnold."

"Oh, my, Arnold. How can you remember the names of all Mr. Jensen's grandchildren?" his mother asked.

Nicholas Christina

Kimberly

Jonathan

...ny, Sarah, Laura ...Mark, Joshua

Jeremy, Stacy

Lisa

...nne, Paul

Amber, Andrea

Ryan, Adam Daniel

Arnold

"It is easy," Arnold told her. "Mr. Jensen has pictures of all his grandchildren with their names written by them. And, of course, I am his grandchild, too. He always tells me he likes me very much, so I adopted him." Arnold was so happy that even his eyes were smiling.

The next day Arnold went over to see Mr. Jensen. It was the same time he always went, right after lunch.

"How are you today, Arnold?" Mr. Jensen asked, just as he did every day.

"I am fine. And how are you today, Mr. Jensen?" Arnold asked, just as he did every day.

"I am very happy today, Arnold," Mr. Jensen said with a smile. "My granddaughter just had a baby girl, and she named her Amy. I am now a great-grandfather!"

"Oh," said Arnold sadly as he started naming all of Mr. Jensen's grandchildren. This time he ended with ". . . and Amy." He did not name Arnold at all. Mr. Jensen had room for twenty-five in his big heart, but Arnold did not think he could possibly have room for twenty-six.

"Come here, Arnold," Mr. Jensen said.

Arnold walked over to Mr. Jensen with his head bowed.

Mr. Jensen pulled up Arnold's drooping chin so he could look in his eyes. "You know, Arnold, there is always room in my heart for you. You are very special," Mr. Jensen said.

"I am?" asked Arnold eagerly.

"Yes, Arnold, you are. You are my next-door-neighbor grandchild, and that is special. We can see each other every day, and we are good friends."

"That's great!" Arnold shouted.

"So would you do me a favor and name my grandchildren again?" asked Mr. Jensen.

"OK," agreed Arnold with a big smile. This time he ended with "and Amy . . . and Arnold."

Who Should Ride the Donkey?

Retold by Cindy Fritz

Many, many years ago there was a chubby old man named Hodja. Hodja was the wisest man in all of Turkey.

One day Hodja and his son went on a short trip. Hodja's son sat on the donkey. On the way they met some villagers coming in the opposite direction.

"That's today's children for you," they said. "The son rides on a donkey and lets his poor old father walk."

When the people had gone, the boy insisted that his father take his place on the donkey. Hodja mounted the donkey, and his son walked at his side. They met some more villagers.

"Just look at that," they said. "There is a full-grown man riding on the donkey, while his poor little son has to walk."

"The best thing to do," said Hodja, when the people had disappeared from sight, "is for both of us to walk. Then there can be no arguments."

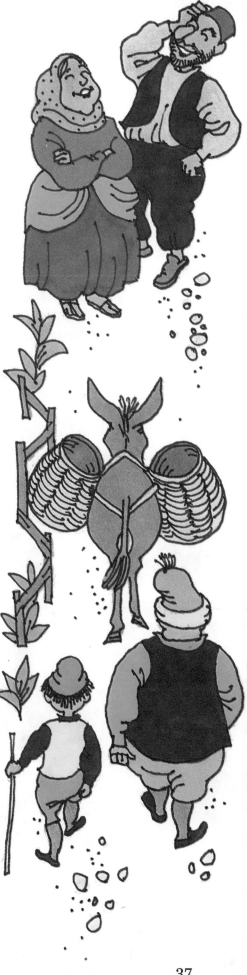

So they continued on their short journey, walking behind the donkey. It was not long before they met another group.

"Just look at those fools," the people said, laughing and pointing to Hodja and his son. "They plod along in the burning heat of the sun, and their donkey takes it easy."

After they had gone, the son turned to his father. "What should we do now? Whatever we do is wrong in someone's eyes."

The wise Hodja said to his son, "Since you can never please all of the people all of the time, it is best to do what you believe is right for you and the ones you love."

With that, Hodja helped his son get back up on the donkey, and they finished their trip the same way they had started it.

37

The Legend of the Red Bird

A Cherokee tale retold by Bonnie Highsmith Taylor

In the First Times, everything had life. Wind, fog, rain, shadows—even sunbeams.

One Sun Child, as sunbeams were called, loved going into the mountain forests where the Cherokee children played.

Sometimes Father Sun would say to this Sun Child, "Today you shall spread your rays across the prairie." Or, "This is a good day for you to go into the deep canyon where the great river runs."

But Sun Child would beg, "Oh, please, Father, let me go to the forest. It is so dark there. The children need my light."

Father Sun would always give in.

Nearly every day in the springtime Sun Child warmed the young flowers that bloomed in the woods. He wakened the ladybugs from their winter sleep. He listened to the laughter of the children.

In the summer Sun Child danced with the butterflies. He sparkled on the ripples of small streams where the children cooled their feet. He was happiest in the summer, for he could come to the forest every day.

In the autumn Sun Child raced with the red and gold leaves as they made their way, twirling and fluttering, to the ground. He warmed the children's chilly fingers and noses in the cool mornings.

But when winter came, Sun Child was sad, for only once in a while could he go to the forest and watch the children play.

Father Sun tried to explain. "You must be patient. The Fog Children, the Wind Children, and the Snow Children must have their turns."

"But in the winter the flowers do not bloom," cried Sun Child. "All the birds leave and go to the warm south. The forest is dark and gloomy. The children need me to brighten the cold winter days." He sighed. "I wish I could stay in the forest always."

"You shall have your wish, my child," said Father Sun.

Suddenly the Sun Child found himself in the forest. But what was this? He was covered with feathers—beautiful red feathers! They glistened on his wings and rose in a handsome crest on his head. He was a bird!

Now he could stay in the forest always. When the other birds flew south for the winter, he would stay behind to brighten the forest. And no one would ever know that this red bird, the cardinal, was once a sunbeam.

Amy's Box

By Linda Daldry

"**A**my," Daddy called. "Come see what I brought home with me." Amy quickly hurried to see what was inside the big box he was holding. But the box was empty. Amy looked puzzled. "What is it for, Daddy?" she asked.

"Why, it's for you, to be whatever you want it to be."

Every day Amy played with her box. Sometimes she hid inside and jumped out at Daddy when he came home from work. But mostly she liked to pretend it was her very own house. She colored windows on the side and a door in front.

One day when Mommy was busy washing windows, something unusual happened. A big lion came to visit Amy's box. Amy didn't like lions. So she ran to Mommy for some help.

"Mommy, there is a lion in my house!" she cried.

At first her mother didn't listen. But when Amy insisted, Mommy said, "Amy, when a lion comes to visit, there is only one thing you can do. You must firmly tell the lion to leave your house and go back to the wilds where he belongs."

Amy did as she was told, and much to her surprise, the lion left without a word.

But Amy's problems were just beginning. No sooner had the lion left than a big brown bear came to take its place!

"Mommy! Mommy!" Amy shouted as she ran to the kitchen for help. "There is a bear in my house!"

This time Amy found her mother hanging curtains, but she stopped long enough to reply calmly, "Amy, when a bear comes to visit, there is only one thing you can do. You must firmly tell the bear to leave your house and go back to the woods where he belongs."

Amy did as she was told, and again her visitor left without a word.

It was not long, though, before Amy was back once again. "Mommy," she cried in great excitement, "now there are three monkeys in my house!"

But this time Mommy replied, "Amy, when monkeys come to visit, there is only one thing you can do. You must ask them to join you for tea."

Amy smiled a great big smile and did as her mother suggested. The three monkeys happily accepted her invitation.

So Amy helped Mommy slice some bananas and fix some tea while the monkeys chattered among themselves. Then they all ate together.

When they had finished, the monkeys thanked Amy and went back to the jungle where they belonged. Then Amy and Mommy washed the dishes together.

The Fisherman and His Wife

An old tale retold by Miriam Biskin

A fisherman and his wife lived in a humble cottage. He loved their home, but she hated it. She often said so.

One day the man went out fishing. Suddenly, something tugged at his line, and he pulled hard. Up came a huge salmon! To his amazement, it spoke.

"I am a king under a wicked spell. Let me go and I will reward you."

The fisherman was a kindly man. Quickly, he unhooked the fish, and it disappeared into the green foam.

He couldn't wait to tell his wife about his adventure. "How foolish," she complained. "Go back for your reward." She sobbed so loudly that he couldn't rest.

Next day he sailed out to sea. He shouted over the waves.

"Splendid fish, splendid fish, please grant my wish."

The fish appeared out of the green foam.

"My wife wants wealth."

"So be it."

When he returned, the woman had bags of gold. But still she grumbled. "This cottage is ugly."

Again the fisherman sailed out to sea. He shouted over the waves.

"Splendid fish, splendid fish, please grant my wish."

The fish appeared out of the green foam.

"My wife wants a splendid house."

"So be it."

The fisherman was amazed at their new home. A mansion! It was framed by green lawns, and inside was fancy furniture.

But still the woman grumbled. "A kingdom," she said. "I want a kingdom."

"Wife, I don't want to be king."

"Well, I want to be queen," she demanded.

Once again he sailed out to sea and shouted over the waves. "Splendid fish, splendid fish, please grant my wish."

The fish rose out of the green foam.

"She wants a kingdom."

"So be it."

Slowly, the fisherman returned home. Slowly, he opened the great door. His wife sat on a throne. She wore a fancy gown. On her head a diamond crown glittered.

But still she grumbled. "Husband, I want the sun and the moon and the stars."

"It's a mistake," he said.

"Go, or I will have you beheaded."

He sailed into the darkness. He called into the wind.

"Splendid fish, splendid fish, please grant my wish."

The fish rose out of the foam.

"My wife desires the sun and the moon and the stars."

"Enough!" The fish's voice boomed. The lightning flashed and the thunder roared. The fisherman trembled.

When he arrived home, all the riches had disappeared. His wife sat by the fire in the old cottage. She wept and he wept. But there they lived forever after.

Oona the Whale

By Willow Ann Soltow

Oona was a whale who lived in Cape Cod Bay. Every day she swam past white farmhouses and past a lighthouse with a red roof. Every night she floated drowsily past jetties that kept the waves from beating too hard against the shore.

Each morning the lobsterman called out to her on his way to his lobster traps. "Good morning, Oona!" he would cry from his black boat. Oona would splash her tail loudly in the water just to say hello.

Oona loved the bay and the land around it. She loved the brightly colored rowboats that lined the shore. She loved to wake up to the squawk of noisy sea gulls. Oona had many friends. Most of them lived beneath the surface of the water on the ocean floor. Oona liked to dive down into the water to visit them. Sometimes she dived down to have a talk with Crab or to visit with shy Octopus.

Oona could not stay under the water for long, however. Whales need

air to breathe, just as you and I do. Oona had to come back to the surface of the water every so often for air.

One day Oona was enjoying the warm sunlight when a sea gull flew by.

"I'm very, very busy," squawked the gull. "Can't stop to talk. Simply can't. Well, perhaps just for a moment, since you insist."

Oona had not insisted, but she was much too kind to say so.

"I've just finished building my nest," the sea gull told her.

"What is a nest?" asked Oona.

"Silly," answered the gull, "a nest is a home. It's a place of your own. I'm going to raise a family there." She cocked her head and looked at Oona. "Whales don't have nests, do they?" she asked.

"No, they don't," said Oona.

"That's too bad, Oona," the gull said. "I'm sorry you have no place of your own."

The sea gull took one last sad look at Oona. "Well, I must go. I'm very busy." And with that she flew away.

All of a sudden Oona was not happy anymore. She did not care about the sunlight on the waves or the friendly sound of the bell buoy.

"I wish I had a home," sighed Oona. She had never really thought about it until now. "I do wish I had a place of my very own!"

Beneath the water Crab waved a claw to Oona. Oona did not really feel like talking to Crab, but she did not want to seem rude. She took a deep breath and dived.

Crab could tell right away that his friend was unhappy.

"What is the matter?" he wanted to know.

"I wish I had a home," said Oona, "a home of my very own."

Crab thought for a moment. "Now let me see. . . . Why don't you find a home in a pile of rocks the way I do? You can't beat a pile of rocks for a nice, safe home."

"That's a good idea," said Oona. She went to look for a pile of rocks. She looked and looked. She could not find one that was big enough for a whale.

"I'll never find a home," said Oona sadly.

"Pssst! Hey there!" hissed a voice.

"Who's there?" asked Oona.

"Hey! Oona! Over here!" It was Octopus. He was hiding in a clump of seaweed. He was too shy to come out of hiding, so he waved a tentacle instead.

"Looking for a place to stay? How about a seaweed home?" he asked. "That's really the best kind of home there is." And he showed her how easily he could disappear into his seaweed.

"I see what you mean," said Oona. She went to hunt for a clump for herself. She hunted and hunted. Finally she found a very large clump of seaweed, but it was far under the water in the deepest part of the bay. Oona could stay there for only a short time before she had to go to the surface and breathe. What good is a home where you cannot stay as long as you want?

"I'll never find a home," she said sadly.

The lobsterman passed Oona on his way home. He waved to her, but she did not splash her tail in reply. She was too sad. She watched his black boat follow the sunset into the shore. She watched as he got out of his boat and went into the clean white farmhouse where his family and a hot dinner were waiting for him.

"I am the only one with no place to go. I am the only one without a home," sobbed Oona. "Oh, what shall I do?"

Up popped a shiny blue porpoise.

"What's the trouble?" asked the porpoise. She had to poke Oona with her snout several times before the whale would answer.

"I have no home," said Oona sadly. "I have no home of my own."

"Why, the whole ocean is your home," the porpoise said happily. "Your home is where you are. Wherever *you* are, *it* is."

"The whole ocean," said Oona softly. "The whole ocean is my home. And all the time that I was looking for it, my home was right here."

"A home is where you make it," said the porpoise.

"In the sand," cried the crayfish.

"In the reeds," sang the sandpipers.

"In the deep sea," said the shrimp.

"A home is where you belong," said Oona. And she splashed her tail loudly in the water—just to show how happy she was.

What Happened to Mrs. Picky

By Sue Santore

At first Mrs. Picky said, "I don't want any peas. I don't like food that is green." Then she said, "I won't eat carrots or sweet potatoes because they are orange." Every day Mrs. Picky refused to eat more and more different foods. She became thinner and thinner.

Mr. Picky, who did all the cooking because Mrs. Picky worked during the day in a big office downtown, was upset. "You don't like my cooking! You won't eat anything anymore."

"I'm sure it is very good," replied Mrs. Picky, picking at her food. "But I just can't eat things that are green, orange, brown, white, or pink."

One Saturday morning when Mrs. Picky was getting dressed, she said to Mr. Picky, "Would you look at this dress! And this and this!"

None of her clothes fit. They were all too big. She put on a blue dress with a white lace collar, folded the dress over in front, and tied a scarf around her waist. "There, that looks better," she said.

Mrs. Picky grabbed her new red-and-gold umbrella, just in case it rained, and slipped downstairs on the banister. "I think I'll go for a long walk today. I should be back by lunchtime," she told Mr. Picky.

"All right, dear," called Mr. Picky from the kitchen. "We're having Spanish rice and cauliflower."

"Orange and white! I can't eat that," cried Mrs. Picky as she slammed the door.

Mr. Picky sighed as he watched his wife walk down the street. "She is becoming a shadow," he said to himself.

"I haven't had a good walk in months," said Mrs. Picky as she strolled briskly down the street. She looked toward Bear Mountain. There were dark clouds hovering around the top of the mountain. "It's a good thing I brought my umbrella," muttered Mrs. Picky. She placed her large handbag on the ground and used both hands to open her umbrella. She clutched the umbrella in one hand, slipped the handbag strap over her shoulder, and off she walked.

"What a friendly breeze," said Mrs. Picky as a small wind came up. The wind grew stronger, and the trees bent and rustled. Mrs. Picky's hair blew against her face and across her eyes. The umbrella lifted in the strong, whirling wind. Mrs. Picky held tightly to the umbrella. It lifted again and slowly carried her into the air.

"Oh, help," called Mrs. Picky. The umbrella rose higher and higher. Now she was above the tallest trees. "Oh, help! Help!" screamed Mrs. Picky, but she was so high no one heard.

As she went whirling up the side of the mountain, skimming over the treetops, Mrs. Picky gritted her teeth. She said, "I always wanted to see the top of Bear Mountain, but not this way." Mrs. Picky floated all around the mountain. Finally the wind grew weary of playing. It blew the umbrella back toward town with little, soft puffs.

High over the houses glided Mrs. Picky. "Hey there," she called, "I'm up here." But everyone was eating lunch, and no one heard her.

She grabbed at the church steeple as she floated past but missed and almost lost the umbrella. There was a tall flagpole just ahead. Mrs. Picky said, "Here's my chance." She grabbed the top of the flagpole with both arms and legs. Just then the wind stopped, and the umbrella fell clunking on the ground below.

Shuddering, Mrs. Picky remarked, "What if I had clunked?" She tightened her legs around the flagpole and asked herself, "What can I do now?" After thinking for a moment, she plunged her hand into her purse and brought out a hammer. "I always knew this would come in handy," she said with much satisfaction.

Bang! Bang! Bang! went the hammer against the flagpole. "Help! Oh, please help!" called Mrs. Picky. She shut her eyes tightly without looking down and banged loudly again.

"I will help you," said a deep voice from below.

Mrs. Picky carefully opened her eyes and looked down. A huge gray elephant was reaching up with its long trunk. Mrs. Picky leaned toward the elephant, who lifted her gently down to the ground.

"What is an elephant doing in the middle of town?" asked Mrs. Picky.

"My zoo keeper forgot to lock my cage door, and I decided to take a walk," replied the elephant. "My name is Junie Jumbo. What are you doing on a flagpole in the middle of town?"

Mrs. Picky blushed. "The wind blew me here. Thank you very much for helping me down."

"Don't mention it," replied Junie Jumbo, "but, if you are tired of this umbrella you threw down, may I have it?"

Mrs. Picky looked away from the umbrella and shuddered. "Of course," she said. "Good-bye, and thanks again."

"See you at the zoo sometime," Junie said and lumbered off.

At the zoo Jack Jumbo said to his wife, "The keeper was looking all over for you. Where have you been, dear, and where did you get that red-and-gold umbrella?"

"You would never believe it," Junie Jumbo replied between bites of hay.

Mrs. Picky scurried home. She quickly washed for lunch and hastened into the kitchen. All the exercise had given her an enormous appetite.

"You are late, dear. What happened?" asked Mr. Picky.

"You would never believe it," Mrs. Picky replied. And she ate everything on her plate.

Cinnamon and Jasper

By Judith Ross Enderle

Cinnamon sat in the circus tent. Her clown mouth turned up, but her real mouth turned down.

"What is the matter?" asked Mr. Ross, the ringmaster.

"The children are not laughing as they used to," said Cinnamon.

"Did you do something different?" asked Mr. Ross.

"No. I did the same act." Cinnamon jumped up. "That could be it! The children have seen my act too many times. I need a new act. I will go for a walk and think."

Soon Cinnamon came to the dining tent. "Maybe I could juggle eggs," she said. "But I do not know how to juggle." She thought of broken eggs. "That might be funny, but it would also be a mess and a waste. No, eggs are not a good idea."

She walked on. She passed the makeup tent. "A big powder puff! Clouds of powder . . . No. Powder might make the children cough. I do not want them to cough. I want them to laugh."

Next Cinnamon came to the animal tent. She went inside. "An animal in my act. That is a fine idea," she said.

Cinnamon spoke with the animal keeper.

"The only animal that is not busy is the little pony, Jasper," said the animal keeper. "But you do not want him. He is a stubborn pony. He cannot be trained. Others have tried and tried."

"Maybe he needs another chance," said Cinnamon. "Do you have a cart, too? Pulling a cart should not be too hard for him."

"Yes, but . . ."

"I will take them both. Please have Jasper ready for the show tonight." Cinnamon could imagine how nice it would be riding into the ring in the pony cart.

"It will not work," said the animal keeper.

Cinnamon did not listen. She hurried to her tent. "A pony and a cart—the children will love it," she said. "It will make my whole act seem new again."

That night Cinnamon sat in the cart as the flying lady came down from the trapeze. "Cinnamon the clown," the ringmaster announced, and the band played.

Cinnamon flicked the reins.

Jasper the pony started toward the center ring.

50

Cinnamon could hear the children clapping. She waved.

Suddenly Jasper stopped.

The children were quiet.

"Oh no!" said Cinnamon. "The animal keeper warned me." She flicked the reins harder.

Jasper the pony went a few more steps. He stopped again. Cinnamon climbed from the cart. "This is not what I planned," she said. She went up to the pony and pulled on him. He did not move.

Cinnamon sighed. She walked toward the center ring.

The children laughed. Cinnamon wondered what was funny. She looked back. Jasper was right behind her. She ran. Jasper ran. She stopped suddenly. Jasper stopped and nudged her. She did a clown fall. Jasper whinnied.

Cinnamon got up and waved her arms as if she were angry. Jasper shook his head.

The children laughed and laughed.

"That was wonderful," said Sam, the strong man, when Cinnamon and Jasper left the ring.

"Marvelous!" cried Mr. Ross, the ringmaster.

"How did you teach him so fast?" asked Fiona, the flying lady.

"I did not teach him," Cinnamon said. "The animal keeper was wrong. Jasper is not a stubborn pony. Jasper just wants to be a clown. We will be a team from now on."

Doodles Plays Tag

By Jolene Mick

Doodles was the biggest goose on Granny's farm. He had a nice place to sleep, plenty to eat, but nothing to do.

He waddled around the farm, poking his beak into nooks and crannies. He hissed at the younger geese, ruffled his feathers, and waddled some more.

"I wish there was something fun to do," said Doodles to himself. "Something exciting."

Suddenly Doodles noticed a lot of noise coming from Granny's yard. Being a curious goose, he decided to waddle over and see what was going on.

Doodles peeked through the fence around Granny's yard and was very surprised at what he saw. There were several children, all of them running, squealing, and laughing.

Doodles got very excited as he stood there peeking through the fence at the children. But then he realized that everyone was teasing and running away from one little boy.

Now Doodles didn't know that the children were playing a game called tag. He only knew that the little boy was trying his best to catch the other children, but couldn't.

"That little fellow looks as if he needs some help," thought Doodles. "And I'm just the one to help him."

Quick as a wink Doodles hopped up on a tree stump, flapped his wings, and went over the fence with a loud *honk!*

The children were startled to see Doodles come over the fence flapping his wings and honking. They shrieked and ran off in every direction with Doodles right behind them.

"What fun," Doodles sang to himself as he chased first one child and then another. "I haven't had so much fun since I chased the old hens out of the chicken house."

Just then the kitchen door banged open and out came Granny, shouting and shaking the biggest straw broom Doodles had ever seen.

"So you think it's fun to scare the children with all your honking and flapping around," Granny shouted at Doodles as she came toward him with the huge broom.

"Uh-oh," thought Doodles as he stood very still with fright. "I wasn't trying to scare anyone. I was just trying to help the little boy catch the other children."

Just then the little boy who had been trying to catch the other children came running up to Granny.

"Oh, Granny," he cried, "please don't hurt the silly old goose. I don't think he meant to scare anyone. I think he just wanted to play."

Granny looked at the little boy, then she looked at Doodles. Slowly she began to chuckle. "You know," she laughed, "I believe you're right. Trying to play tag sounds just like something Doodles would do."

"OK, Doodles," said Granny as she shook her finger at him. "You can play with the children, but next time don't scare everyone so much when you want to play."

So all day long Doodles had the best time of his life playing tag with the children. He honked and flapped his wings as he chased them around the yard. His little heart was so happy Doodles felt he would pop open.

Soon it began to get dark, and Granny called the children inside. The little boy stooped down and put his arms around Doodles.

"Maybe tomorrow you can play hide-and-seek with us," he said.

Doodles didn't know what hide-and-seek was, but he had a feeling he'd like it.

Tracy Turtle's Ice

By Sally Lucas

The sign on the window said "Help Wanted." Tracy Turtle was happy that she could read. She wanted that job. She liked to work.

Tracy went into the store. "I need a job," said Tracy. "Some people say I am slow, but I am a good worker."

Mr. and Mrs. Polar Bear looked at each other. Mr. Bear said, "I like this turtle. She looks like a hard worker. But what if she is too slow?"

Mrs. Bear said, "I hope she is slow. When Ryan Rabbit worked here, there was ice cream spilled all over. It's not good to be too fast. Let's give this turtle the job."

So Mr. and Mrs. Polar Bear taught Tracy the job. One scoop of ice cream cost one nickel. Two scoops cost two nickels. Three scoops cost three nickels. Tracy Turtle was happy she could count.

Mrs. Polar Bear showed Tracy the ice-cream tubs. The brown tub had chocolate ice cream. The white tub had vanilla. The yellow tub had banana. The red tub had strawberry ice cream, and the green tub had mint. Tracy was happy she knew her colors.

Tracy worked hard. When she got tired, she could take naps by hiding her head inside her shell. Customers liked to knock on Tracy's shell when they wanted service.

One Saturday Mr. and Mrs. Polar Bear said, "Tracy, you are such a good worker that you do not need us here. We are going to take a vacation. We will be back in a week."

On Sunday Tracy was busy. All the squirrels in town seemed to like ice cream on Sunday. But they wanted only chocolate ice cream. Monday, Tuesday, Wednesday, Thursday, and Friday were busy days, too. Many customers came into the store, but they wanted only vanilla ice cream. Soon the brown and white tubs were almost empty.

Tracy was sad. Nobody was buying the other flavors of ice cream. "I need to get new customers," Tracy said to herself.

On Saturday Tracy got an idea. She made a big sign. It said
Rainbow Ice Cream—5¢
Tracy practiced making a rainbow cone. Slowly, very slowly, she put a dab (not a scoop) of each ice cream in a cone. Soon all the birds nearby flew into the store to buy rainbow cones. "We love rainbows," chirped the birds.

Cream Store

Just then Mr. and Mrs. Polar Bear returned from vacation. They saw the big sign, "Rainbow Ice Cream—5¢." They saw all the customers eating rainbow cones. "Oh, my! We will scare the birds away," said Mr. Bear. "Let's stay away another week."

"Let's stay away forever," said Mrs. Bear.

"Yes, yes," said Mr. Bear. "Let's make Tracy Turtle the manager of our ice-cream store. She can read. She can count. She knows colors. But, best of all, she can think of new ideas!"

The next sign Tracy made was the best sign of all. It read

Tracy Turtle's
Ice-Cream Store

Too Many Rocks

By Karen Ivon Cecil

Amanda liked rocks. When she went to the park or walked down the alley, she always took her wagon. She filled it with rocks and brought all of them home.

"You have too many rocks," said her sister, Judy. "You have rocks in your closet and rocks on your desk."

"I like my rocks," said Amanda.

"My fish are much better," said Judy. "They swim and breathe and eat. But your rocks just sit."

"But I don't have to feed them or clean a fish tank," said Amanda. "I'd rather have rocks."

One day her family had a picnic in the country. Amanda found smooth, round rocks in a little stream. She took them home in the picnic basket.

"You have too many rocks," said her brother, Peter. "You have rocks in your chair and rocks on your dresser."

"I like my rocks," said Amanda.

"My flowers are much better," said Peter. "They grow and bloom. But your rocks just sit."

"But I don't have to water them or pull weeds around them," Amanda said. "I'd rather have rocks."

One weekend her family went camping near a lake. Amanda found big, rough rocks and small, shiny rocks along the shore. She hid as many as she could in her sleeping bag and took them home.

"You have too many rocks," said Amanda's mother. "You have rocks on the floor and rocks on the bed."

"I like my rocks," said Amanda.

"Your rocks are lovely," Mother said, "but where are you going to sleep?"

Amanda liked her rocks, but she didn't want to sleep with them. "Couldn't I put them in the living room?"

"No," said Mother. "No rocks in the living room. If no one needs them, we will have to throw them out."

Amanda began to think. Surely someone needed her rocks.

Amanda put all her small rocks in a box. She found Judy feeding her fish.

"Your fish are nice," Amanda said, "but they need something."

"What?" asked Judy.

"My rocks." And she put a layer of shiny stones at the bottom of Judy's fish tank.

Judy watched the fish swimming in the tank. "My fish like your rocks. And I do, too."

Amanda carried her big rocks outside. She found Peter pulling grass from his flower bed.

"Your flowers are pretty," Amanda said, "but they need something."

"What?" asked Peter.

"My rocks." And she started making a border of rocks around Peter's flower bed.

Peter watched her for a moment. Then he began to help. "This will keep the grass out of my flowers. They like your rocks. And I do, too."

Amanda had one rock left, a sparkly white one with a stripe of red. She found her mother working at her desk.

"Judy's fish needed my rocks," said Amanda. "So did Peter's flowers. And you need this one." She put her last rock on Mother's desk to keep the papers from blowing away.

Mother smiled. "I like your rock. But didn't you keep any for yourself?"

"No," said Amanda. "But when I go for a walk, I'll take my wagon."

Mike's Rosie

By Chester Aaron

"Quiet, please."

The crowd in the bleachers grew silent.

Behind Mike, high above the field, the judges leaned over their score sheets, their binoculars focused on Rosie, the border collie sitting at Mike's right heel. At the far end of the field five sheep ran down the truck's ramp. Rosie trembled. Mike gave her ear a loving scratch.

This time the loudspeaker was soft. "The sheep are yours."

"Rosie," Mike whispered, "go by."

The collie leaped into action, running so fast her feet never seemed to touch the grass. Coming up behind the sheep, slowing but not stopping, she moved them forward.

As the sheep, still grazing, approached the first obstacle, Rosie dashed back and forth, crouching, lying low, staring, dashing again. The five ewes were not even aware they'd been driven through the narrow gates. Not one tried to break from the pack.

The second obstacle, a series of gates, had eliminated two champions earlier in the afternoon.

Rosie seemed to know the sheep's thoughts before they did. A black-

and-white ball of constant motion, all eyes and ears and feet, she dominated the sheep so thoroughly she might make a perfect score. Would she triumph? Could she become the new Grand National Champion? Mike was uncomfortable. This was too easy. Something had to go wrong. He shifted the plastic whistle in his mouth so he'd be ready, just in case.

The sheep were bunched so tightly now they seemed tied, body to body. Mike signaled Rosie once, when she crowded the sheep as they approached the chute. He sent her back a few paces and stayed her, to ease her tension.

"Rosie's still a young dog," his father had told him just before the trials started. "She gets excited. You stay relaxed, son. You help *her* relax."

Mike knew that his mother and father, sitting in the bleachers, were checking their watches. They hadn't expected Rosie to get this far, to be one of the three finalists, competing with national champions—but here she was.

They had given Mike the spotted pup four years ago, when he was eight. "You train her," his mother had told him, "you work her, you love her." He had done just that for four years, staying close to his parents in the fields whenever they worked the sheep, pairing Rosie with one or both of the two older, wiser dogs. Mike and Rosie had grown older and wiser together.

A groan in the audience brought him back to Rosie. He'd broken the first rule: He'd let his mind wander. Thinking about the past, he hadn't seen the big ewe break from the flock and race across the field.

As if she had a gear she'd never used before, Rosie, in a sweeping run, charged after the rebellious ewe, cutting in front of it, bumping it lightly, turning it back toward the pack that milled near the entrance to the chute. Then a second ewe broke away, trotting toward the green grass in center field. The remaining three waited near the chute.

Rosie extended her run to circle the second ewe, which pivoted to keep its tormentor in sight, stumbled over its own feet, and fell. Rosie, snarling, was after it, but the ewe scrambled up and returned to the chute entrance.

The five sheep were together again, and Rosie, not even stopping to pant, moved, head low, eyes staring, inching all five sheep closer to the final obstacle, the chute.

The chute consisted of walls without a roof. Any dog that could move its sheep between those walls could be relied upon, in the field, to move sheep through a chute and into a truck. This last, difficult trial had already reduced other champions to has-beens.

Mike checked his watch. He'd give Rosie five seconds. If her instincts proved wrong, he'd have to intervene.

He did not have to. It was all over in fifteen seconds.

The five sheep had entered the chute. Suddenly the big rebel whirled and leaped. Rosie went up in the air, caught a bit of wool, and flipped the big sheep onto its back. It lay there, eyes closed. The sheep's eyes opened to see other eyes staring, the eyes of a small black-and-white dog that must be thinking itself a wolf. When the ewe rose to its feet and ambled meekly into the chute, the bleachers shook with cheers.

Rosie pranced at Mike's side as he led her out to receive her trophy. She sat obediently at Mike's heel, trembling slightly as she looked downfield toward the parked truck. Mike reached down to scratch her ear, but she continued to stare at the truck, waiting. She glanced up only once, when Mike accepted her trophy.

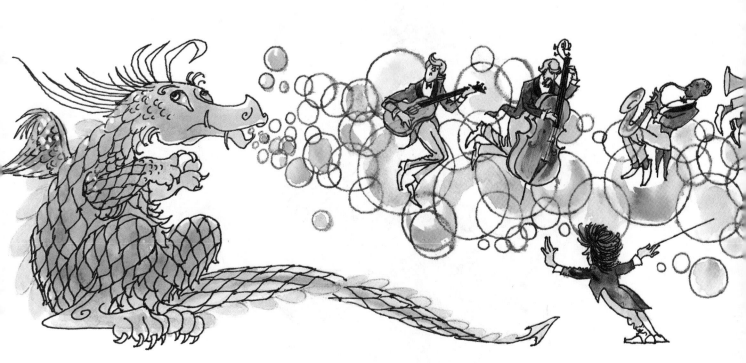

Why We Don't See Dragons

By Susan Goodman

A long time ago, when the world was very much the same as it is today—except younger—dragons lived almost everywhere.

From time to time dragons would travel into people's towns to see a movie or to have picnics in the park. They would walk down the streets smiling at people. They were trying to be friendly, but people were afraid that the dragons were smiling at the thought of eating them for breakfast.

Although dragons live for a thousand years or so, their feelings get hurt rather quickly. So one day, after a hundred years of reading signs that said "Dragons, Go Home," Dexter Dragon started crying.

Dewberry, the oldest dragon, found him sobbing. She had also visited town that day, and had been kicked in the knee by a little boy who didn't like dragons.

"Enough is enough!" she cried after hearing Dexter's story. "Something must be done about the way people treat dragons." She put

little Dexter on her tail and limped back home.

"We need a meeting," she told the other dragons. "A meeting of all the dragons in the world." She asked the sea gulls to fly to every corner of the earth and spread the news.

Soon dragons of all kinds and sizes started to arrive. First came the dragons that breathe fire, then the dragons that breathe bubbles. Then came the dragons that breathe clouds and, finally, the dragons that breathe rainbows.

"I've called you together to help solve our problem with people," Dewberry said. "We can't live with them if they don't like us. How can we change their minds about us?"

The dragons sat and talked. They stood and talked. They ate and talked. They talked and talked for sixty-two days, which is only a moment in dragon time.

Finally, a big dragon named Dreedle popped up with an idea. "People don't trust us because we're not like them," he said. "We can't become people, but we can show them just how friendly dragons can be."

"That's it!" cried Dewberry. "Let's use our dragon breath to be friendly and help people."

The dragons were so happy that they started to dance. They danced so much that they began to breathe hard and fast. Soon the air was filled with flames and bubbles, clouds and rainbows.

The next day a fire-breathing dragon went to town and offered to help cook hamburgers for the annual Independence Day Barbecue. But after eating a few hamburgers himself, the dragon burped and burned down half the stores on Main Street. People chased him out of town with fire extinguishers.

Then a bubble-breathing dragon went to town and got a job blowing bubbles behind a band on television. But when the band played her favorite song, the dragon got excited and blew so many bubbles that soon the musicians were floating on a sea of bubbles near the ceiling. The bandleader ordered the dragon off the stage.

Next a cloud-breathing dragon went to town and blew out some wonderful clouds shaped like fuzzy animals. But people were afraid of the funny-shaped clouds and shouted angry words at the dragon. That made the dragon cry. She cried so hard that the clouds filled with rain and flooded the town. The dragon swam sadly home in her own tears.

"I'll go next," said the rainbow-breathing dragon. "Surely people will like me." He walked into town, bent his head way back, and breathed out such a beautiful rainbow that people just stood around staring at it. But not some bank robbers, who sneaked into the End-of-the-Rainbow Bank. While everyone else was staring at the sky, the robbers had no trouble getting away with the money. The mayor gave the dragon one hour to get out of town.

It was time for another meeting. So Dewberry called the dragons together.

"What are we going to do?" she cried. "We've tried and tried, but nothing we do makes people like us."

Dexter Dragon stood up. "I have watched us try hard to please others," he said. "But people still aren't happy, and neither are we. Perhaps the whole idea is wrong. Perhaps all we can do is be ourselves. Then at least we will like ourselves. Maybe someday people will learn to like us, too."

The dragons cheered. This was true wisdom. They decided to find a corner of the world where they could live happily by themselves. The dragons still live there today. They're waiting for people to find them and like them just for being dragons.

The Bugler of Bonkersville

By Janette Gentry

Mr. Bangles was the bugler of Bonkersville. He blew his bugle in parades. He blew his bugle when the mayor made speeches. He blew his bugle when dignitaries came to visit, and he blew his bugle at town picnics. Mr. Bangles dearly loved picnics.

But when Mr. Bangles played, the grown-ups put their hands over their ears. They did not like to hear the bugler.

But the children did. They liked to hear Mr. Bangles blow his bugle. So each morning Mr. Bangles shinnied up the tall, tall flagpole in the center of Bonkersville. He sat in a little seat on top of the flagpole and blew a tune—just for the children. The tune had a bouncy beat, and when the children heard it, they bounced right out of bed. Their parents never had to fuss to get them up.

At bedtime . . . well, that was a different matter. The children never wanted to go to sleep.

They whined. They cried. They wanted to hear umpteen bedtime stories. They asked for umpteen glasses of water.

Finally, the mayor called a meeting. "What can we do about these bad habits our children have developed?" he asked the parents.

The parents shook their heads. They had tried just about everything.

Then one mother said, "Let's ask Mr. Bangles to play his bugle at bedtime. Maybe the children would bounce *into* bed the way they bounce *out* of bed in the mornings."

It was worth a try.

But Mr. Bangles shook his head sadly. "My poor legs are too weak. I can't climb the flagpole twice each day!"

"We'll help you," the parents told him. So that night they went to the flagpole to give Mr. Bangles a boost. In fact, they gave him several boosts. But each time—*ziiiiiip!* Mr. Bangles came sliding right down again. *Plop!*

"Mr. Bangles needs a tall, tall ladder," someone suggested. But in all of Bonkersville not one ladder could be found that would reach to the top of the flagpole.

"What I really need," said Mr. Bangles, "is a big balloon. I could float to the top of the flagpole."

"Great idea!" said the mayor. "We must make Mr. Bangles a balloon."

So everyone set to work. They blew up lots of little balloons and paper bags. They tied them all together to make one big, bunchy balloon. Then they tied it to Mr. Bangles's suspenders.

Slowly, slowly the big balloon began to rise. Up, up, up went Mr. Bangles. He reached the top of the flagpole. Suddenly— *Whooooooosh!* A big gust of wind blew him away.

Over the rooftops sailed Mr. Bangles. Over the water tank, the schoolhouse, and the church steeple. Mr. Bangles was afraid he was heading for the moon.

"Help! Help!" he yelled. And then he heard an awful sound—*Shhhhhhhh.* Air was escaping from his bunchy balloon. He drifted slowly back to the ground.

"We give up," everyone said, and went home.

Everyone gave up but Mr. Bangles. He wouldn't give up. "There's got to be a way," Mr. Bangles told himself over and over. Suddenly, a thought came to him—no one had asked the children if they had any ideas. Mr. Bangles called a meeting of the children.

"Can you think of a way to help me shinny up the flagpole twice each day?" he asked them. They had already discussed it.

"We think we have a solution to the problem," said one boy. The children all nodded in agreement.

The next day Mr. Bangles sent notes to all the parents. *Come to the flagpole early in the morning,* the notes read. *I have a surprise for you.*

And what a surprise it was! Mr. Bangles sat in his seat on top of the flagpole. He sat beneath a bright yellow umbrella. He wore green sunglasses and a purple straw hat. Tucked in his hatband were three dill pickles, four bananas, and six peppermint sticks. From Mr. Bangles's seat hung a picnic basket. He was eating a sandwich and drinking pink lemonade.

The parents all started talking at once.

"He's having a picnic!"

"On top of the flagpole!"

Mr. Bangles grinned happily. "It was the children's idea!" he shouted. "They know I just love picnics. I can have a picnic all day, every day. I'll come down after I blow my bugle at bedtime."

"Hoorah for Mr. Bangles! Hoorah for the children!" shouted all the people.

That night, while the bugler played his bugle, the children snuggled down in their beds to listen. They lay very still, for the tune didn't have a bouncy beat. It was slow and dreamy. And in no time they were fast asleep.

And Little Leonidas

By Ivy O. Eastwick

Once there lived in the Ungeley Bungeley Jungle a family of lions—Father Lion, Mother Lion, Loopy Lion, Lucy Lion, and the youngest one of all, Little Leonidas.

Each day they would go for a walk through the Ungeley Bungeley Jungle. There they would say a polite "Good morning" to any tigers, panthers, and elephants who happened to be passing their way. They would say a very special "Good morning" to their friends and cousins, the dotted, spotted leopards.

The youngest of the dotted, spotted leopards used to hide themselves away in the shadows of the tall trees, where they were not easily seen. Loopy and Lucy had fun "spotting" them, and Mr. and Mrs. Lion joined in the fun by adding up the number of spottings each of their children made. Sometimes Loopy made as many as seven spottings, Lucy seldom made more than three, while as for Little Leonidas—he had no success at all. He just never could see where his dotted, spotted cousins were hiding.

One morning, while the Lion family was out for a walk, Little Leonidas stopped to gaze up at a tall scarlet orchid because it was so beautiful. His family, intent on their spotting game, went on through

67

the Ungeley Bungeley Jungle and did not notice that he was no longer with them. In no time at all Little Leonidas was lost. He ran this way and that way, trying to find his family. Where could they be?

All at once he heard a furious billowing-bellowing, hunting-grunting, lumbering-stumbling sound nearby.

He looked around in alarm and saw Old Ly-No, the bad-tempered rhino. There was only one thing to do, thought Little Leonidas, and that was to run as far and as fast as possible. His parents had warned him about Old Ly-No the rhino, who was every bit as cruel as he was ugly. A baby lion would be no match for HIM.

Little Leonidas ran. Ly-No the rhino ran, too, lumbering and stumbling but every bit as fast as Little Leonidas.

"Help! Help! Somebody help me!" squeaked Little Leonidas, for in his fear he had lost his voice and only a squeak would come out.

Suddenly he heard a voice whisper, "Here. Over here."

He looked all round but could see no one.

However, he ran in the direction of the voice. Suddenly, to his great joy, he realized that he was among lots of spots—the spots of his friends and cousins, the dotted, spotted leopards.

They quickly surrounded him, and in half a second he, too, was just a part of their dappley, shadowy, dotted spottedness.

Old Ly-No gave a grunt of great disappointment, for now he could see nothing but dappled tree shadows. He lumbered away deep into the jungle.

Then the leopard family guided Little Leonidas safely back to where the lions were seeking their lost cub.

And was Little Leonidas glad to see them again?

Well, what do YOU think?

But after this, whenever the golden young lions and their dotted, spotted cousins, the leopards, played their hide-and-seek game, Loopy would manage six or seven spottings; Lucy, three or four spottings; while as for Little Leonidas . . . yes, you've guessed . . .

Little Leonidas could spot as many as ten at a time. Easily.

Henry Has the Life

By Eileen Spinelli

Henry D. Penrose was a dog with a pedigree. He lived in a fine stone house with white marble steps and red velvet drapes on every window.

His owner, Professor Randolph Penrose, was quite rich.

Each morning Henry was driven to Obedience School in a long black limousine.

Each afternoon he was fed two grilled lamb chops for lunch.

Each evening he fell asleep in his fur-lined basket in front of the fireplace.

On Saturdays he was groomed at Miss Fifi's Shop. And on Sundays he accompanied the professor to the park, where a classical orchestra played soothing music and the grass was cool and fragrant.

Professor Penrose would stroke Henry's shiny coat and say, "You have the life, Henry, my boy!"

And Henry certainly had to agree.

Then one day it all changed. Just. Like. That.

Professor Penrose received a telegram offering him a chance to dig for dinosaur bones in Idaho. For one entire year.

There was only one problem. The telegram stated quite firmly in the largest letters possible: NO PETS ALLOWED!

The cook, Mrs. Washburn, agreed to take Henry to her home until the professor returned.

Professor Penrose hated to send Henry to live on the other side of the city. There were no marble steps or red velvet drapes on Mrs. Washburn's property.

But Henry was buttoned into his red plaid coat and driven to the Washburn residence.

Henry stepped out of the limousine. He was so shocked that his ears stuck out like two car doors.

Such an untidy home he had never seen. It was all he could do to maintain a sense of dignity.

He was picking his way through the toys on the muddy front steps when a tumble of children spilled onto the porch and scooped him up. Before you could say "one-two-kalamazoo," Henry was deposited in a sea of soap bubbles in the Washburn bathtub.

Each time he tried to jump out, little hands pushed him back in.

"Don't be too rough, children," said Mrs. Washburn. "Henry isn't used to such fun."

Dinner that evening was a big steamy ham bone. Bits of cabbage fell from it as one of the children tossed it to Henry. What! thought Henry. No plate?

He wondered if he'd ever see a grilled lamb chop again.

By bedtime Henry was exhausted. His fur-lined basket had been left behind. Where would he sleep?

Just then two of the children carried him off to a room with three bunk beds.

"Henry's sleeping with me!" announced one child, pulling him to one bunk.

"Oh no! Henry's sleeping with me!" protested another, yanking him toward another bunk.

A third child elbowed his way in, and Henry flopped to the floor.

Before he could crawl under one of the beds, a pillow fight broke out.

Thwack! A pillow smacked into Henry's face. He barked. Loud!

Mrs. Washburn came scurrying down the hallway. The children scattered into their beds.

"Why, Henry!" scolded Mrs. Washburn. "You never barked like that before! Quiet down, or the children will never get to sleep!"

On Sunday there was no park or classical orchestra. No cool and fragrant grass. Just the Washburns' backyard with its dandelion clumps and creaky swings and a fort made out of empty cardboard boxes.

The children wrestled with Henry. They scratched his ears and tied an old red Christmas ribbon round his neck. They tried to make him chase the cat next door. Baby Washburn even kissed him—a big, sloppy, wet, strawberry-lollipop kiss, right on the nose.

Later, when Baby toppled over onto Henry's tail, they both cried, "Yeeeeoooooooow!"

Mrs. Washburn poked her head out of the back door. "Don't hurt Baby, Henry."

Days, weeks, months passed.

Henry learned to put up with pillow fights and strawberry kisses. He learned to ignore the neighbor's cat and to wriggle Christmas ribbons off his neck. He even learned to eat steamy ham bones.

And then one day everything changed. Just. Like. That.

Professor Penrose returned.

The long black limousine came to take Henry back to the professor's fine stone house.

The Washburn children gathered on their front porch. Tears streamed down their cheeks. "Good-bye, Henry," they sniffled sadly. "Good-bye!"

That evening, after being groomed by Miss Fifi (who kept sighing over the tangles in his coat) and after being fed two plump, perfectly grilled lamb chops (in his own monogrammed dish), Henry climbed into his fur-lined basket in front of the fireplace.

He yawned. He laid his head on his front paws. He closed his eyes.

But he did not go to sleep.

Something was wrong. Everything was so quiet, so peaceful. *Too* quiet. *Too* peaceful.

Henry climbed out of his basket. He nudged open the front door and headed down the road to the Washburn house. At first he walked properly, as he had been taught. Then he ran.

When he arrived, he scratched at the door.

Mrs. Washburn opened it. "Why, it's you, Henry. Welcome home!"

Henry dashed up the stairs and into the children's bedroom. It was dark.

Thwack! A pillow smacked into his face.

Henry ducked under one of the beds. He smelled the faint scent of strawberry, and as he drifted off to sleep, he was thinking, You have the life, Henry, my boy. You have the life.

The Three Sleepers

By Benjamin Elkin

Once there were three lazy bears.

"If I sat on a sharp stone, I'd be too lazy to stand up," said Bear One.

"If I found lots of honey, I'd be too lazy to lick it," said Bear Two.

"I'm too lazy to tell you how lazy I am," said Bear Three.

"All right," said Bear One. "Let's find a nice, lazy place and have a nice, lazy sleep."

Then the three bears went off into the mountains. First they lay down under a shady tree. But that spot wasn't lazy enough. In the tree there was a nest full of birds who went *tweet! tweet! tweet!* all the time.

Then the three bears lay down under another tree. But the leaves of the tree were too busy. The leaves kept rustling and whispering in the wind.

The bears found a green field with no birds to tweet and no leaves to rustle. But there was a busy cricket who kept going *chirp! chirp! chirp!*

At last they found a secret cave hidden behind bushes. This cave seemed just right. There were no birds to tweet, no leaves to rustle, and no crickets to chirp.

"Now for a real rest," said Bear One.

"Now for a nice nap," said Bear Two.

"Now for a silent sleep," said Bear Three.

The three lazy bears made themselves comfortable. In one moment they were fast asleep.

Hours passed. The sun went down, and the moon came up. Still the three bears slept. The next day passed, and another day. Yet the bears slept on.

The days grew into weeks. The weeks grew into months. Summer passed and autumn came. Leaves turned red and yellow. Children picked fat pumpkins for Halloween. In the sky, ducks flew south. In the woods, the squirrels gathered nuts. And in the cave, Bear One opened her eyes.

"What time of the year is this?" she asked. But Bear Two and Bear Three were sound asleep, so Bear One closed her eyes again. In a moment she was fast asleep.

Again, the days came and went. Days grew into weeks and weeks into months. Now it was winter. White snow covered everything. Children and their fathers and mothers came for Christmas trees. Other children made a snowman holding a broomstick. In the woods, rabbits made tracks in the snow. And in the cave, Bear Two opened his eyes.

"How should I know what time of the year it is?" he said. But Bear One and Bear Three were sound asleep, so Bear Two closed his eyes again. In a moment he was fast asleep.

Once again, the days came and went. Days became weeks, and weeks became months. At last it was spring. The grass was green again. Children flew kites in the wind. In the woods, baby birds opened their mouths to be fed. And in the cave, Bear Three stood up.

The other two opened their eyes in surprise. "Where are you going?" they asked.

"I'm leaving!" said Bear Three. "You two keep talking about what time of year it is. How can I sleep with so much talking?"

"We're sorry," said Bear Two.

"We won't talk anymore," said Bear One.

The three bears made themselves comfortable again. Soon they were fast asleep.

From then on, the seasons came and went. Outside, the birds sang in summer and the winds blew in winter. But inside the cave, all was quiet. And the lazy bears slept on and on.

So, the next time you are in the mountains, be sure to walk softly. Maybe those three lazy bears are still in their secret cave, enjoying their long, long sleep.

How Elephant Found

By Marileta Robinson

They say that long ago, in the beginning of things, animals had no voices. The bird, the wolf, and the lion all went about their business as silently as stones.

But after a while all that silence made the animals feel lonely. They decided that they should find voices for themselves. So each animal went out to find the sound that would be its voice.

The bird heard the rain singing on the pebbles. *Twitter! Twitter! Peep!* That was the voice she chose.

The wolf heard the wind howling in the tall trees. *AOOOO!* He chose that voice.

The wild pig liked the sound her foot made when she pulled it out of the mud. *Oog! Gluck!* That was the sound she chose.

The lizard chose the sound a shadow makes when it slides across a rock.

The giraffe listened to the clouds blowing across the sky. She chose that sound.

The lion listened for a long time. "I must find a sound that is great enough for the mightiest of beasts," he said to himself. Finally, in the

Her Voice

middle of a fierce storm, he heard the thunder shake the ground. *GRRAAH!* That was the sound he chose.

But Elephant listened and listened with her great ears and could not find any sound to suit her.

She heard the wind whisper in the dry grass.

She heard a branch crack under her foot.

She heard the river splash and gurgle when she waded in to get a drink.

But none of these sounds was right for her.

She heard a giant tree crash in the forest.

She heard a boulder rumble down a hill.

She heard a waterfall roar into a canyon.

But these sounds were not right for her either.

So Elephant walked sadly through the forest and listened to all the other animals squeaking and chirping and barking as they practiced their new voices.

The monkey was sitting up in his baobab tree, watching her. "Maybe I should cheer up poor Elephant," he said to himself.

Quickly he slipped down from his tree.

Quietly he slipped up close behind Elephant.

Hai! He yanked Elephant's tail as hard as he could.

Up went Elephant's trunk! Back went Elephant's ears! And out of her mouth came a most amazing, never-before-heard sound! *HAROOOMBA!* It knocked the monkey head over heels.

Elephant twitched her tail and gave a satisfied nod. "There it is," she said. "That is the sound I've been listening for. It is just right. And to think it was inside me all the time!"

Elephant trotted off, happily practicing her new voice.

And the monkey, back safe in his baobab tree, grinned and made a sound like two branches rubbing together. *Eee-eee-eee! Eee-eee-eee!* But he never played a trick on Elephant again.

The Houses on Harmony Lane

By Lloydene Cook

There were six houses on Harmony Lane.

Mr. Moose lived in the first house. The Raccoon family lived in the second house. Mr. Fox lived in the third house. Miss Possum lived in the fourth house, and Mr. and Mrs. Squirrel lived in the fifth house. Nobody lived in the sixth house.

All six houses were exactly alike. They were each painted yellow. They all had white shutters and blue-checkered curtains at the windows. There were red geraniums growing in each flower bed, and there was one maple tree planted in exactly the same spot in each front yard.

Everyone was happy on Harmony Lane until Miss Owl moved in.

The first thing Miss Owl did was replace her red geraniums with marigolds and chrysanthemums.

The neighbors watched and whispered among themselves.

"We've always grown geraniums on Harmony Lane," Mr. Moose sniffed.

"Geraniums are nice," Miss Owl said. "But I also like marigolds and chrysanthemums."

The next thing Miss Owl did was to plant a persimmon tree in her front yard.

"Nobody else has a persimmon tree on Harmony Lane," the Raccoon family complained.

"I'll share my persimmons with everyone," Miss Owl said.

One day Miss Owl took down her blue-checkered curtains and hung red-striped ones.

"No one on Harmony Lane has ever had red-striped curtains," protested Mr. Fox.

"I made them myself," Miss Owl said. "Aren't they cheerful?"

Then the worst thing happened. Miss Owl painted her house green.

"But all the houses on Harmony Lane are yellow," Miss Possum whined to Miss Owl.

"Now there is a green house on Harmony Lane, too," Miss Owl said with a smile.

Later that day all of Miss Owl's neighbors held a meeting at Mr. and Mrs. Squirrel's house.

"Oh, whatever shall we do?" cried Miss Possum.

"Miss Owl's house is different from all the rest," said Mr. Squirrel.

Mr. Moose scratched his head. "Maybe it's good to be different," he said. "I've always wanted to have a blue house with yellow shutters. I think I'll paint my house, too."

"We have always wanted to have some apple trees," Mrs. Raccoon said. "We'll plant some tomorrow."

"And I'm going to sew some new curtains," Mr. Fox said. "I have always wanted green curtains."

"Well, I'm going to build a white picket fence around my house," said Miss Possum.

The next day all the neighbors worked on their houses. Miss Owl helped, too. She helped Mr. Moose paint his house blue with yellow shutters. She helped the Raccoon family plant apple trees. She helped Mr. Fox sew some green curtains, and she helped Miss Possum build a white picket fence.

When she came to Mr. and Mrs. Squirrel's house, she found them sitting under their maple tree. Their house was still yellow with white shutters and blue-checkered curtains.

"We decided not to change a thing," said Mrs. Squirrel.

"That's a wise decision," said Miss Owl. "You will feel most at home in a house you like."

Prairie Dog's Coffeepot

By Marileta Robinson

One morning Jerry Prairie Dog woke up in his cool, clean hole in the ground. "A-a-a-h!" he yawned, and stretched his legs. "I'm going to have a big cup of hot, black coffee!" He jumped out of his bed of rabbit fur and built a fire in the stove. When the fire was crackling, he started to go outside to put some water in his blue-and-white spotted coffeepot. But where was his coffeepot?

Was it under the bed? He looked under the bed. No, not there.

Was it on the shelf? He looked on the shelf. No, not there either.

Was it behind the stove? He looked behind the stove. No, it wasn't there.

Where was it? Jerry Prairie Dog sat down to think. Then he remembered. Yesterday Mrs. Rabbit had borrowed it. Maybe it was still at her house.

Jerry ran to the top of his hole and looked around. He saw Mrs. Rabbit working in her garden. "Good morning, Mrs. Rabbit," Jerry called. "Do you have my blue-and-white coffeepot?"

"Oh, dear," said Mrs. Rabbit. "No, I don't. Mrs. Goat came over yesterday and said she needed it badly. I gave it to her."

"Well," said Jerry, "I'll go see if she has it." And he ran off to Mrs. Goat's hogan.

Mrs. Goat was not there, but her children were playing out in front. "Hello," said Jerry. "Have any of you seen my blue-and-white coffeepot?"

"No, we haven't seen it," said the older goat children. But the smallest one said, "Yes, I saw it, Mr. Prairie Dog. I was playing with it down by the stream bed. I think I left it there. I'm sorry, Mr. Prairie Dog." He started to cry.

"Don't cry," said Jerry. "I'll just run down and see if it's there." And he ran off to the dry stream bed.

Jerry looked and looked, but he couldn't find his beautiful blue-and-white spotted coffeepot anywhere. "Hum!" said Jerry sadly, and he sat down on a rock. Just then the smallest goat child ran up.

"Mr. Prairie Dog," he said. "I found your coffeepot. Come see." They both ran down the dry stream bed until they came to a fence. There stood Miss Cow.

"Oh, Jerry Prairie Dog and Tommy Goat," said Miss Cow. "Look what I've found. Isn't it beautiful? It's just what I've always wanted." Jerry saw his blue-and-white coffeepot sitting on the fence. It was full of flowers.

"It's very nice, Miss Cow," said Jerry. Then he and Tommy Goat walked away and sat down under a tree.

"What are you going to do, Mr. Prairie Dog?" said Tommy.

"I have an idea," said Jerry. "Do you have any paint?"

"Yes," said Tommy, "I think so."

"Good. Go back home now. I'll come over soon."

So Tommy Goat went home, and Jerry Prairie Dog ran back to his hole. He found a tall tin can in a box of trash and ran with it to Tommy's hogan.

"Here's the paint," said Tommy Goat. "And here's a brush."

"Thank you," said Jerry.

First they washed the tin can, and then Jerry painted it a beautiful bright blue. When the blue paint was dry, he splashed spots of white paint all over it. At last it was ready. "Let's give this to Miss Cow," he said.

When they got back to the fence, they found Miss Cow fast asleep beside the coffeepot. Quietly Jerry took out the flowers and put them in the blue-and-white can.

"I think she will like that," Jerry said. Then he said good-bye to Tommy Goat and started back home, happily swinging his coffeepot.

But Jerry Prairie Dog wasn't going to get his big cup of hot, black coffee that easily. Oh no! What was that on the other side of the yucca plant just ahead? A big brown furry paw—Coyote's paw!

"Oh, there you are, Prairie Dog," Coyote growled. "You're just in time for my prairie-dog stew."

Jerry Prairie Dog didn't wait to hear any more. He ran as fast as he could to a little hole in the side of a hill. The hole was so small that he had to drop his coffeepot outside. He ran deep inside, under the hill. Coyote snuffled and scratched at the hole. But the hole was between two rocks, and Coyote couldn't make it any bigger. With a little whine he trotted away.

Jerry Prairie Dog came out slowly. He picked up his coffeepot. Then he heard a hissing voice inside the pot say, "SSStay out! Thisss isss a niccce houssse for a sssnake to sssleep in!" Jerry dropped the pot again. He didn't want the snake to bite him. He went back down in the hole.

Pretty soon he heard somebody coming. It was Grandfather Sheep.

Jerry wriggled out of the hole and whispered to Grandfather Sheep what had happened to his coffeepot.

"Well, well," said Grandfather Sheep. "I have an idea," and he whispered in Jerry's ear.

Jerry laughed and said, "That should work."

First they picked up some sticks and put them in a pile. Then Grandfather Sheep said in a loud voice, "There! Let's go home to get some matches so we can make a fire." And then, even more loudly, "NOTHING TASTES QUITE AS GOOD AS COOKED SNAKE!"

Then Grandfather Sheep and Jerry Prairie Dog ran behind a rock to see what would happen.

Very soon the snake came out of the coffeepot and slithered away as fast as he could. Cooked snake didn't sound good to him!

Jerry ran over and picked up his coffeepot. "Thank you, Grandfather Sheep." He laughed. "Come to my house, and we'll make a big pot of hot, black coffee!" And they did.

Sylvester Woodchuck
Goes to Sea

By Marjorie R. Sheffer

Sylvester Woodchuck dragged his mother's washtub and his bed quilt down to the pond. It was much too nice a day to stay inside. The sun was shining, and a breeze was blowing. It was a perfect day for sailing.

"Where are you going?" called Mother Woodchuck. "I thought you were going to clean your room."

"I'll do it later," Sylvester promised. "Anyway, my quilt needs airing."

He jammed a stick into the washtub for a mast. He tied his quilt to the stick for a sail.

"My quilt will get a VERY good airing today," he said to himself. There was just enough room in the washtub beside Sylvester for a bag of sandwiches and a bottle of lemonade.

"Sailing, sailing, over the bounding main," sang Sylvester. He ate the sandwiches and drank the lemonade. The washtub bobbed up and down on the waves. Sylvester dozed in the sunshine. This was better than cleaning his room.

A strong wind swooped down from the sky. With a great puff it snapped off the stick mast, and the quilt went flying away in the air, flapping like a giant bird. The tub bounced up and down in the rough water, rolling poor Sylvester from side to side.

Finally the tub stopped with a hard bump and didn't move at all. Sylvester peered over the edge to see what had happened. The tub was caught by its handle on a tree stump in the middle of the pond. Sylvester jerked this way and that, but he was stuck. A duck came swimming by to see what all the clatter was about.

"Can you help me, please?" said Sylvester. "I can't move."

The duck pushed the tub with her bill and fluttered her wings, but nothing happened.

"Sorry," she quacked, and swam away to dive for insects.

Sylvester leaned over the side. Two large carp swam up to the tub.

"Can you help me get loose?" Sylvester asked.

"We'll try," the answer bubbled up. The fish butted the tub with their broad, stubby heads. But it did not move, and they glided away. No one else was in sight.

"I'm stuck here forever," Sylvester cried. If only he had a pencil and paper, he could write a note and send it ashore in the lemonade bottle. If only he could get home, he would clean his room until it sparkled. He felt very sorry for himself.

A cross voice on the other side of the stump said, "This stump belongs to us beavers. You'd better leave, Mister!"

"I would leave if I could," said Sylvester. "But my boat is stuck here, and I can't get it loose by myself."

There was some splashing, and a beaver appeared, wet and shining. "You mean your washtub is hooked on our stump?"

Sylvester nodded. He no longer felt like a bold sailor.

"No problem," said the beaver. He went to work gnawing the stump where it stuck through the washtub handle. The chips went flying, and the tub was free at last. "There you go," said the beaver. He swam behind the tub, nudging it to shore, then turned around and swam back without waiting to be thanked.

Sylvester saw a little spot of blue lying in the meadow and trotted around the pond to rescue his quilt. He was very tired when he reached the house.

"Where have you been all this time?" said Mother Woodchuck.

"Airing my quilt," Sylvester mumbled. "And, um, doing other stuff."

"It does smell fresh and nice," said Mother Woodchuck, sniffing at the quilt. Then she looked stern. "But your room is still messy. Go upstairs and clean it."

Upstairs, Sylvester looked at the heap of toys. One by one he put them on the shelf until there was a clear spot in the middle of the room. He yawned, then crawled into bed and pulled his quilt over him. It smelled of sweet meadows and sunny days.

He was snoring when Mother Woodchuck peeked into his room. She saw a note pinned on the quilt: "Dear Mother, I will finish cleaning my room tomorrow. Love, Sylvester P. Woodchuck."

First Choice

By Cheryl Mays Halton

"Hi, Mom," Franny said as she ran into the kitchen. "Sorry I'm late, but I stopped by to see the puppies at Mrs. Morton's. They're the most beautiful little Irish setters I've ever seen."

"How old are they now?" Mother asked.

"Four weeks old today. In just two more weeks I'll be able to bring one home," Franny said, smiling.

"You'll have to work awfully hard to earn enough money in just two more weeks," said Mother.

"Yes," Franny agreed, "but Mrs. Johnson said I could cut her grass Saturday, and Dad promised to have some extra chores for me, too."

Franny had been saving her money for a long time—ever since last summer when her parents had said she could have a dog if she saved enough money to help pay for it.

An Irish setter was the only kind Franny had ever wanted. Her brother, Mack, teased her, saying it was because Irish setters had red hair just like hers. That wasn't true, of course. It was because Irish setters were big and sleek and friendly and liked to play outdoors. It was also because her older cousin Laura had one and said they were the best dogs in the world. It seemed to Franny that everything Laura said was always right.

The next day Franny stopped in to see the puppies just as she did every day.

Mrs. Morton unlatched the gate to the pen so Franny could play with the puppies. "Which one do you want?" she asked. "I have six puppies and eight people wanting them. I've told everyone that you get first choice."

"I haven't made up my mind yet," Franny answered. "But I'll decide tonight, for certain."

Franny walked home slowly along the creek. She needed time to decide which puppy she wanted.

Franny was thinking of the puppies when, suddenly, she heard a soft, high-pitched noise coming from a pile of small branches by the side of the creek.

There it was again. A whimper. It seemed to come from under the pile of brush. Franny lifted a branch carefully and then another and another. Still she didn't see anything. But now the whimpering was louder and more excited. Franny lifted another branch. There was a hole, and at the bottom of the hole was a little black-and-white dog. It was not much larger than a puppy, and it was thin, dirty, and full of burrs.

"You poor little mutt," Franny said. She jumped down next to the little dog and lifted it to her shoulder. The little dog was shaking with delight.

"I'd better take you home and get you some food and water. You look awfully hungry."

Franny walked toward home, carrying the little dog. As she reached her yard, she saw her mother standing on the porch.

"I thought you wanted an Irish setter," Mother said, "and here you come with a little black-and-white dog."

"I still want an Irish setter, Mom," Franny said, "but I found this dog in the woods, and he looks hungry. I'll feed him, and then he'll probably find his way back home."

"He certainly looks happy that you found him," Mother said. "He hasn't quit licking you for a minute."

After the dog had eaten his dinner, Franny brushed the dried mud out of his coat. By the time she had finished, the dog looked a lot better. Franny patted him for a moment and went inside.

"Where's your friend, Franny?" Mother asked.

"He's on the back porch," said Franny. "Maybe he'll go home if I leave him alone for a while."

But after dinner Franny looked out the window, and there was the little dog sitting on the porch, just waiting for her to come out again.

Franny opened the door and bent down to pet the little dog. Up he hopped, his tail wagging furiously, and his tongue reaching for Franny's cheek.

"I guess you're lonesome," Franny said. "I'll play with you for a while, but I'll have to go in soon. I have homework to finish. Besides, I have to decide which Irish setter I'm going to take."

The next morning at breakfast Franny peeked out the kitchen window, and there sat the little dog, waiting patiently for her to come outside.

Franny opened the door and stepped out on the porch. The dog barked happily and ran around and around her, jumping delightedly as Franny tried to pet him. The little dog was having such fun that soon Franny was laughing and coaxing him to greater excitement. She 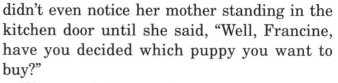 didn't even notice her mother standing in the kitchen door until she said, "Well, Francine, have you decided which puppy you want to buy?"

"I'm not going to buy a puppy, Mom," Franny said.

"But I thought you had your heart set on an Irish setter," Mother said.

"I did—but so do lots of other people. And this puppy has his heart set on me."

The Long Ride

By R. E. Richards

David Jay arose and stumbled bleary-eyed to the long, wooden-plank breakfast table where a steaming plate of fried eggs was waiting. He gobbled down his breakfast, snatched up a water flask and packet of beef jerky, and rushed outside.

In the dim morning light David could just barely make out the lanky form of Mr. Thompson, the station keeper, who stood holding the reins of a horse in front of the log station house.

From off in the distance came the rolling thunder of hoofbeats as a rider approached at full gallop. The dusty, buckskinned rider, a young man of about nineteen, pulled up his horse alongside Mr. Thompson. The rider sprang from the saddle, pulled leather mail pouches from the back of his horse, and slipped them over the saddle of the horse that Mr. Thompson was holding.

In an instant David leaped into the saddle of the fresh horse and was off at full speed, just as the sun began to peek above the edge of the flat Nebraska plains.

David had just begun his daily race against time. He was a Pony Express rider. The Pony Express was a cross-country mail company, and its riders carried pouches of mail between St. Joseph, Missouri, and Sacramento, California. For months David had carried the mail back and forth across the Nebraska territory in this "relay race" on horseback.

After an hour's ride David approached the first swing station. Swing stations were spaced about fifteen miles apart along the Pony Express route. Here the riders could exchange tired horses for fresh ones. David dismounted and handed the reins of his sweating, exhausted horse to the station keeper, who put the mail onto a new horse. Moments later David was again flying along the trail.

Late in the day, David pulled up to the Fort Kearny express station, sore and tired from his long ride. Karl, the station keeper, rushed out to meet him.

"David, we've got a problem," explained Karl. "Charlie, the next rider, was attacked by bandits and wounded. I don't have another rider to take the mail to Cold Springs."

David knew that, above all else, the mail must get through.

"I'll make the trip," he replied quickly.

Although David dreaded riding another eighty miles on the trail, he was glad to get a chance to go to Cold Springs. Old Hank Torrens was the Cold Springs station keeper. Hank had been a good friend of David's family. It was Hank who had taught David to ride.

David stayed in Fort Kearny only long enough to eat a hot meal and catch his breath. Back in the saddle, he rode westward toward the setting sun.

Soon it became dark, and David had to slow his pace. But the moon was full, and it was fairly easy to follow the trail.

By the time David arrived at the fifth and last relay station, his body ached from the more than seventeen hours he had spent in the saddle. He longed to stop and rest, but his common sense told him that if he stopped now, even for a short while, he would never be able to get up and finish the ride.

For miles, David rode on through the darkness. Suddenly, he heard the sound of hoofbeats following close behind. Mail bandits! David spurred his horse into a gallop. The Pony Express horse, carrying only a thin boy and twenty pounds of mail, had the lighter load, and the sound of the riders behind it began to grow fainter and fainter.

Just about the time that David knew he had put a safe cushion of distance between himself and the bandits, his horse stepped into a hole. The animal stumbled and fell, pitching David headlong onto the trail. Shaken but unhurt, David ran back to remount and continue his ride. The horse had already gotten to its feet, but it was limping badly.

The boy's heart sank when he realized that the injury was too serious for the horse to be ridden.

David led the crippled horse off the trail, while he listened anxiously for hoofbeats. But the cool night air was still and silent. David slid the mail pouches off the horse's back and draped them over his own shoulders. He would come back later for the horse.

Back on the trail, David started running in the direction of Cold Springs with the precious pouches bouncing against his chest. On and on he went. The mail pouches began to feel like thousand-pound weights forcing him to the ground.

Even after his last ounce of strength was gone, David's legs kept moving—driven only by the desire to complete his mission. Finally, he could go no farther. His tired body collapsed onto the cold ground.

In his dazed, weary mind, David thought that he was in a cabin, resting comfortably by a warm, crackling fire. But the sound of approaching hoofbeats quickly snapped him back to his senses. Had the bandits caught him at last?

A rider stopped nearby. David clutched the mail tightly. But he soon relaxed when he found himself peering into the kindly, smiling face of Old Hank.

To Paint with Words

By Diane Burns

Twisted Grass leaned against his rimrock shelter. He loosened his grip on his warm antelope robe. The rising morning fog no longer made his young bones ache. Old Wise One, squatting straight-backed beside him, felt the sun's warmth, too. Turning blind eyes toward the river canyon, Wise One listened sharply. He heard the rushing waters. "The river races deep," he said. He spoke in the tongue of his people— the Tukudeka, or Sheepeaters.

Wise One sees with his ears, Twisted Grass thought bitterly. He does not need me to be his eyes.

The last wisps of cloud lifted. There, below them, rushed the mighty Agaimpaa river, leaping in its swollen spring dance. Twisted Grass felt a knot in his stomach at the sight of the wild water. And there, like tiny ants clinging to the cliffs above the river, came Strong Horn and the other young men from the Sheepeater family. They must reach the weathered caves safely. Only the brave dared to tease Agaimpaa. Only the brave dared to cross Agaimpaa while it raged with high water.

The men carried tools and mud-colored paint. In the caves they would sketch bright red drawings of successful Sheepeater hunts and trading days.

Twisted Grass sighed. He could have gone with the men to paint cave pictures. Strong Horn had asked him. What an honor that would have been for Twisted Grass, a boy of twelve summers! Yes, he was young, but no one drew *tuku*, the mountain sheep, better. Even Strong Horn knew that Twisted Grass was the best artist in the clan. But Wise One had not let him go. Twisted Grass swallowed hard, forcing down the bitterness.

"Twisted Grass paints for me with words this season." Wise One had spoken calmly, and it was agreed.

Wise One was head of the clan. Before his blindness, he had always taken care of his people. No one had stalked more cougar. No one knew raging Agaimpaa the way he did. "Wise One is brother to Agaimpaa," the Sheepeaters said. And no one had traded more carefully with neighboring tribes. Sturdy sheephorn bows made by Tukudeka, Twisted Grass's people, were prized by others. No people but Tukudeka tanned animal skins so soft. Twisted Grass stirred with pride. Tukudeka lived in the wild mountains with only coyote dogs for company. Yet they were safe during trading times with shrewd Wise One to help them.

Twisted Grass glanced at Wise One. Such a strong face! Like an arrowhead chipped from stone. Who would guess that the aged eyes saw only blackness now?

Wise One is my friend, Twisted Grass reminded himself. He saw me painting in mud as a child, gave me tools. He taught me, encouraged the others to let me paint. And for what? Is this how my training ends?

The boy sighed, but Wise One did not notice. Blind Wise One had journeyed to this rocky overlook without missing a step along the narrow game trail. Across the loose shale he had marched as if he could see every rock. Twisted Grass had scarcely been able to keep up. "He does not need my eyes," the young Tukudeka repeated to himself.

"Paint for me with words," Wise One had said. "As if you are smearing color on rock, tell me what you see." He had settled himself against the rimrock to wait for Twisted Grass's word pictures.

Twisted Grass hunched tighter in his blanket-skin, as if afraid that his rebellion would escape for Wise One to hear. I paint on stone, the boy argued silently. I do not paint with words. Wise One sees every cliff and swirl of the river in his mind. Of what use am I to someone who has seen all, who is brother to Agaimpaa?

A nagging thought tugged at his mind the way he'd seen his little sister pull at their mother's skirt. Wise One cannot see *now*, came the thought. He must have eyes, *your* eyes at this moment, if he is to be part of *this* time and place.

Twisted Grass narrowed his eyes against the sun's glare. His friends still climbed upward. They want me. They need me. He ached.

Wise One wants you, too, came the calm reply. He needs you. He picked you.

He picked me! The surprising thought made Twisted Grass blink. It is true! Wise One picked *me*. Not Strong Horn, not the experienced hunters. Why me?

And then, suddenly, Twisted Grass knew. Wise One had taught him to paint. He will see what I see because of the words I use. Because of the way I say them. Because we are friends who understand the same beauty.

We understand the same beauty. Happiness settled around Twisted Grass and warmed him like ten antelope blankets. Wise One broke the silence softly. "Tell me what you see, Twisted Grass."

Twisted Grass's heart stirred again with pride. Yes, there is honor in painting cave legends with Strong Horn. But there is also honor in painting word pictures.

With a deep breath, Twisted Grass began: "Wise One, the cave of Strong Horn's choice yawns like a lazy bear. It is the color of a newborn cougar. And mighty Agaimpaa twists below like the great green snake that rattles with anger. Agaimpaa cannot reach Strong Horn. He will be safe in the caves."

One gnarled hand rested lightly on Twisted Grass's thick black hair. Wise One did not smile, but his deeply lined face was peaceful. He is happy, the boy realized. He sees this time and place through my words. It is good!

Twisted Grass went on, choosing his words as carefully as he would choose colors for a rock painting. And as he described the scene to Wise One out loud, Twisted Grass was busily preparing a different scene in his mind—a scene he would someday paint on a cave wall. It would be a special drawing of a young Tukudeka who had once honored his friend, Wise One, by painting a picture of words.

"No Borrowing, Blake!"

By Kathleen Pestotnik

Blake poured himself a second glass of juice and stretched his bare feet across the kitchen chair. It was not just any Friday. It was a no-school Friday. That meant he had the whole day to . . . uh-oh.

The den meeting! He'd nearly forgotten, and it was his turn to bring treats. He'd promised homemade cookies. His mom wouldn't be too happy about that. *She* had school today. She was the teacher half of parent-teacher conferences.

Blake's mother hurried into the kitchen. "James will be here any minute to stay with you. And my conferences will be finished by noon at the latest. We can have lunch together. Anything you need before I go?"

"Could we bake this morning?" Blake asked hopefully. "I have to take treats for Cub Scouts."

His mother groaned. "I wish you had warned me. I'm out of everything."

"Mrs. Easton bakes a lot," Blake said. "Maybe I could . . ."

"No borrowing, Blake! Remember last time when you and James made gourmet fudge? I had to go to five stores to find that special brand of English walnuts you borrowed."

The look on her face as she grabbed her coat and hurried out the door warned him not to argue.

"OK," he sighed. "No borrowing."

Now what? he wondered. He couldn't let the guys down. He dressed quickly and headed for the elevator. Maybe James would have an idea.

But when the elevator door opened, James was not there. The only passenger was hidden behind a huge armload of bulging grocery bags.

"Mrs. Easton? Is that you?" He took the top bag, and sure enough, Mrs. Easton's plump red face appeared.

"Bless you," she puffed. "I never . . . would have . . . made it . . . alone."

"You must be baking today."

"I wish I had time." She sighed. "My grandchildren are coming, and they love homemade cookies."

Blake set the bag in the doorway. "Have a good weekend," he called.

It wasn't fair, Blake thought. Mrs. Easton wanted to bake but didn't have time. He had the time, but . . .

"No borrowing, Blake!" his conscience reminded him.

When James finally stepped out of the elevator, he had a football under one arm. "Hi, James. New football?"

"Better!" He tossed it to Blake. "Take a look."

"Wow, autographed by Roger Staubach!"

"I traded for it—my old watch for this rare football." James grinned. "Pretty good deal, huh?"

A slow smile spread across Blake's face. "Gee, I hope I'm as smart as you when I'm fifteen."

Blake handed back the football and unlocked the apartment door. "Come in. I've got to check something."

He took his mother's recipe box down

from the kitchen shelf and found the card he wanted. One by one, he read off the ingredients and took them from their storage places, setting each item on the counter by the stove. Mom was right, they were out of sugar, eggs, and chocolate chips.

Blake grabbed a pencil and pad from the drawer and figured rapidly. It just might work. He dug a paper bag out of the cupboard, pocketed his list, and started for the door.

James stared at him curiously. "Where are you going?"

"Secret mission," Blake replied mysteriously. "Don't worry. I won't leave the building."

He'd start with Mr. Landon. Mr. Landon lived alone, but he had a real sweet tooth. Then there was Mrs. Garcia and, of course, Mrs. Easton.

He was back in five minutes. "Mission accomplished," he announced, holding up the bulky bag. "Want to bake some cookies?"

"They don't call me Super Chef for nothing." James chuckled. "But are you sure your mom won't mind?"

"It's OK," Blake assured him. After all, it wasn't the baking she objected to; it was the borrowing.

Ten minutes later, the two were up to their elbows in sticky dough and the cookies were ready for the oven.

"We'd better stay right here and watch them," Blake warned. "I want to end up with forty-eight perfect cookies."

It was almost noon when James flipped the last cookie onto the rack to cool. "Tasting time?" he suggested.

Blake shook his head. "Not yet." He took four plastic bags from the drawer and began counting cookies into them. Fourteen in the first bag, six in the second, eight in the third, and twelve in the last. He finished just as he heard his mother's key turn in the lock.

Blake grinned sheepishly at her. "You're just in time."

She sniffed the buttery-sweet aroma and frowned. "So I see. I thought we had an agreement."

"I didn't borrow. Honest!"

"Then how . . ."

"I *traded*. Mrs. Easton swapped chocolate chips for a dozen cookies. Mr. Landon gets six for two eggs, and Mrs. Garcia . . ."

His mother laughed. "I get the message. You found a way to bake without borrowing, and I don't have to make an extra trip to the store. I just hope you can break the news gently to your dad. Chocolate-chip cookies are his favorites, and you've traded them all away."

"Not exactly," Blake said with a sly grin. "I made some for trading, some for treating, and some . . ."

"For eating!" they shouted together.

Little Raindrop

By Marilyn Kratz

"I am tired of being a drop of water," said a raindrop one day. "I look just like all the other raindrops falling from this cloud."

"Oh, I can change you," said the North Wind.

She blew the raindrop higher into the sky. He froze into a tiny ball of ice. Other raindrops froze in layers around him.

"Now you are a hailstone," said the North Wind.

Down fell the hailstone. He melted into a raindrop again. Then the North Wind blew him up into a cold, cold cloud. This time the raindrop froze into a beautiful six-pointed snowflake. He floated down and melted on a freckled nose.

Next, the North Wind divided the little raindrop into many tiny droplets, and he became part of a fog cloud wrapped around a bridge.

"Would you like to be frost on a windowpane now?" asked the North Wind.

"No, I am too tired," the raindrop said. He settled onto a blade of grass to rest.

"What a sparkling drop of dew," said a little girl as she walked by.

The little raindrop just smiled and twinkled back at her.